MITCH

AN EIDOLON BLACK OPS NOVEL: BOOK 5

MADDIE WADE

Mitch
An Eidolon Black Ops Novel: Book 5
by Maddie Wade

Published by Maddie Wade
Copyright © August 2020 Maddie Wade

Cover: Envy Creative Designs
Editing: Black Opal Editing
Formatting: Black Opal Editing

Acknowledgments

I am so lucky to have such an amazing team around me without which I could never bring these books to life. I am so grateful to have you in my life, you are more than friends you are so essential to my life.

My wonderful beta team, Greta, and Deanna who are brutally honest and beautifully kind. If it is rubbish you tell me it is and if you love it, you are effusive. Your support means so much to me.

My editor—Linda at Black Opal Editing. You are always patient and kind and teach me so much.

To Renita McKinney from Book A Day Author Services thank you for making sure I was true to Mitch and Autumn. It is always important to me to make sure I am inclusive of all cultures and ethnic groups and you made sure I did both Mitch and Autumn justice.

Thank you to my group Maddie's Minxes, your support and love for Fortis, Eidolon and all the books I write is so important to me. Special thanks to Paula, Tracey, Faith, Rachel, Carolyn, Susan, Maria, Greta, Deanna, Rihaneh and Linda L, Annemieke, and Alison for making the group such a friendly place to be.

My Arc Team for not keeping me on edge too long while I wait for feedback.

Lastly and most importantly thank you to my readers who have embraced my books so wholeheartedly and shown a love for the stories in my head. To hear you say that you see my characters as family makes me so humble and proud. I hope you enjoy Mitch and Autumn as much as I did.

I am dedicating Mitch to the Minxes.

CONTENTS

Chapter One

Mitch hooked his thumbs in the loops of his pockets as he looked up at the old building in need of a little TLC. Glancing sideways, he nodded up towards the roofline as he spoke to his friend, Nate. "What would a new roof set me back?"

Nate owned a similar property three doors away and had completely renovated it into the large family home it was now.

Nate shoved his hand in his pockets as he stepped back to look up at the broken roof tiles. "Around ten to fifteen grand, I'd say."

Nate worked for Fortis Security, a company Eidolon did a lot of work with, and the teams got on well and socialised together a fair bit too. Hereford wasn't a vast metropolis, so it was expected they would run in similar circles, but it was the fact he and Nate were both snipers that made the two of them tight.

Mitch whistled thinking of his bank balance, trying to do some quick calculations in his head. "That's a decent chunk of change."

Nate nodded. "It is but these properties are solid. It's an investment in the long run."

Mitch looked up again at the sprawling Victorian home that spanned three floors. It had already been split into four separate flats by the previous owner. That meant he could rent three of them out for extra income.

He'd been working for Eidolon for a few years now and was happy there. Hereford was home now, and he wanted to put down some roots, invest in his future, and as Nate's father David constantly reminded him, bricks and mortar were always a good investment long term.

Glancing at the windows which would need replacing, he could see how the property could swallow money if he let it but as Mitch stared silently, he could also see the potential.

"Be nice when it's done up. Most of the work is cosmetic apart from the roof and windows."

Nate chuckled. "Make a nice family home one day too."

Mitch held up his hands with a raised eyebrow, a grin on his lips. "Hey, steady on, I'm too young for all that."

1

"Yeah, whatever, gramps. I need to get back. Skye has to deliver a cake to a bride at the Left Bank and I need to watch Nancy and Noah." Nate held up a hand as he walked up the street.

That was the biggest difference between the two friends. Nate was a devoted family man and at forty-five Mitch was a dedicated bachelor.

It wasn't that he wanted to be, or that he played the field the way he used to in his younger days, just that it had never happened. He'd seen far too many marriages fail in his time as a member of SO19, the Firearms division of the London Metropolitan Police Department. So many relationships had crumbled from the pressures of the job, and he had no intention of forcing one just to satisfy convention.

He would rather wait until he could have what Alex, Blake, Reid, and now Liam had with their women. If that meant it didn't happen, he'd be okay with what he had.

Mitch strolled to the back of the property for one last look before he made his decision. Later that day, his offer on the property was accepted.

Six months later, Mitch was living in one of the top floor flats. Waggs had rented one of the ground floor ones, and Bebe, one of the Zenobi girls, had the other ground floor flat. He'd decided to leave the middle floor for now until he figured out if he was going to increase his living space, but he liked being on the top for now. It suited him having tenants he knew, especially since he'd spent more cash doing it up than he'd intended. That was why the last apartment on the top floor opposite his own was up for rental through an agency. He had little worry he'd end up with a bad tenant with all the hoops people had to jump through and especially with Will, the owner of Eidolon and a tech genius, offering to run background checks on them first.

His phone rang as he was walking into a meeting with the team and he quickly answered it, stepping aside as Waggs walked past him and into the large conference room.

"Yep."

"Mr Quinn, this is Melissa from the letting agency. We have a potential tenant for you."

"Great."

"But they can only view the property after hours."

2

"And?" He moved his hand in a wrap this up gesture even though she couldn't see him.

"We were wondering if you could show them around?"

Mitch sighed, he had no time for this, but he'd be around so he guessed it wouldn't be too much of an imposition. "Yeah, sure. What time?"

"Is eight tonight too late?"

"Nah, that's fine."

"Thank you. I'll let Ms Roberts know."

Mitch hung up and walked into the conference room where everyone was waiting. He clapped Liam on the shoulder as he took the seat next to him. "How are you feeling?"

"Pucker mate."

Liam insisted on using cockney words as a way to irritate the rest of the team who barely understood him half the time, although they seemed to be learning quick enough.

Mitch nodded, glad to see his friend back on rotation and fighting fit again, after the gunshot wound he'd received protecting the woman he loved.

Jack, their boss, banged the table with one hand. "Listen up. We have a few things to cover."

The room grew silent as everyone focused on the job first and foremost.

"Firstly, we've had word from the Palace that the Queen wants to do a tour of the commonwealth next year." Jack flipped a pencil end over end as he spoke. "That means we're up. We need to plan it, visit locations, and prep. Her usual security will continue with the day to day stuff, but this is where we shine, gentleman. We need this contract if you want to keep making money."

"What about the threat inside the Palace? Has Gunner given us anything useful?"

Decker leaned back in his chair, the coolest cucumber in the room, and the most well-dressed. He lived in a suit while the rest of them wore jeans, combats, or training gear. Perhaps it was because as the profiler, his brain was his biggest weapon, whereas the rest of them were more the brawn.

"He's meeting me in two days and says he might have a name for us by then." Jack sat forward. "Any questions?"

3

"You got any closer to hiring a dog unit?" Blake was the one with the most experience in personal protection, having had close contact with the Queen long before they got this contract. He was all in favour of having a K9 unit for the teams. Mitch had to say he agreed, it worked for Fortis well and was the only place they had a real gap in capabilities.

"I'm interviewing candidates with Alex and Decker on Friday."

"What about admin and stuff? I'm sick of getting stuck with that shit," Lopez said.

Mitch threw a ball of paper at his head. "Stop whining, you big baby."

Lopez lobbed it back. "You try doing it and see how you like it."

"Can't, they need my exceptional skill in the field, nerd boy."

"Fuck off, grandad."

Mitch laughed at the dig knowing it was a joke. As the oldest member of the team, he frequently got called gramps and grandad—it didn't bother him in the slightest. "When did forty become old?"

"When did it stop?" Lopez countered, and the guys cracked up as did he.

"Touché."

This camaraderie was why he loved this team; they laughed, they joked, but when it mattered, they would take a bullet to save one another. It was a similar feeling to the one he'd had long ago when he grew up surrounded by his gang, except the current one was highly trained and mostly legal.

Until Eidolon, he'd missed the element of belonging that being part of a crew had given him. It was the only part he did miss though. The rest had been too high a price to pay for his best friend's life. Walking away from the gangs, getting out of South London had literally saved his own life. It was something he'd be forever grateful for, and his mum was the woman he'd always have to thank for it.

As a single mum since his dad's death, she'd worked her fingers to the bone to keep a roof over their heads, and not once had he gone without. But ultimately, it was her grit, her strength to drag him bodily to another area and away from the people who would have cost him his life had he stayed, that was the thing he was most grateful for.

Jack leaned forward on the table catching everyone's attention, holding a room with his authority in such a way nobody realised it half the time. "Well, Lopez, you'll be happy to hear that I've looked at the budget and hired an office admin."

"Thank fuck for that. Tell me she's pretty, with long legs…."

"She's off fucking limits. Aubrey will have my balls if you touch her sister, and anyway, I'm not having you pricks hitting on the office staff and costing me a fortune in legal fees when she sues us."

"Madison? Are you fucking kidding me?" Lopez threw his pen down on the desk, shaking his head.

Madison was a handful to say the least. The team had saved her from a Colombian drug lord after she'd got herself in trouble.

"It's a favour for Aubrey."

Nobody responded to that because everyone loved Aubrey, Will's girlfriend, who was also a local police detective.

"I'm also hiring someone to coordinate logistics for us. Pax has very kindly agreed to help me find someone."

"Pax should come work for us. She'd be awesome." Reid looked at Blake with a raised brow.

"Not going to happen, my friend. She's loyal to Roz. Plus, we'd probably kill each other."

Reid laughed. "True dat."

Pax was the most efficient woman Mitch had ever met, and she'd be a massive asset to the team, but he had to respect her loyalty to Zenobi.

Jack stood from his chair, leaning his hands on the table. "Well, if that's all, we can meet here next Monday and go through a detailed list of jobs when I've met with the Palace."

"Need someone with you?" Mitch asked, not liking the idea of Jack going alone when they knew a threat to the team originated there.

"Blake is coming with me, but a second set of eyes would be good."

Mitch nodded, and everyone stood as the meeting wrapped up. Mitch looked at his watch and figured he had time for a workout before he met the prospective tenant.

That turned out to be longer than expected when he got into a sparring match with Waggs and Reid, and then Alex joined them. Before he knew what had happened, it was seven-thirty.

"Fuck, I need to be somewhere." Throwing his gloves in his bag, he rushed through a shower and shoved his jeans, navy t-shirt, and boots on before jumping in his car and driving the fifteen minutes home.

Pulling up, he noticed a rusted-out Ford Focus parked on the road outside his house and cussed again. He hated being late for anything.

Throwing his bag over his shoulder, he stepped through the front gate and came face to butt with the sweetest ass he'd ever seen, and Mitch had seen his fair share. A sexy woman with long black hair in braids was bent over pulling weeds from his garden.

"You here to see the flat or did I contract a gardener and forget about it?"

The woman instantly turned and flashed him a questioning smile. Forget the ass, her face was even better, with a regal, oval shape, a warm rose gold skin tone, and lush, full lips meant for kissing. The woman tilted her head to look up at him with eyes the colour of autumn leaves, the longest lashes he'd ever seen sweeping over high cheekbones. Her long black hair was held back from her face in a knot, the rest skimming almost to her waist as she moved towards him, hand outstretched.

"Mr Quinn, I'm Autumn Roberts." She waved a hand behind her. "Sorry about that, I couldn't help myself. Gardening is a bit of a passion of mine."

"Mitch."

She frowned adorably while rubbing her hands together to get the soil off them and he fought not to grin like an idiot.

"Sorry?"

"My name is Mitch."

"Oh, I see."

He regarded her, taking in the whole package, and found himself intrigued. This woman was beautiful and friendly, a good start.

"Can I see the property?"

Mitch jumped. "Oh, yeah. Sure." He moved towards the door, feeling like a knobend for staring at the poor woman.

He led her to the stairs and looked back at her as she looked around. "It's on the top floor."

He opened the door and let her go in first, wanting another look at her rear end to see if his assessment had been spot-on the first time. Yes, it definitely had. Her curves filled out those jeans perfectly.

6

Shaking his head, he walked towards the kitchen area. "It's fitted out with new units and appliances. Carpets and laminate are also new, so is the bathroom suite and windows."

Autumn walked to the window and looked out at the long garden. "Do you allow children? The agent wasn't sure."

"As long as they're housetrained and not gonna keep everyone up all night." He'd hoped to elicit a smile from her, wanting to see how she looked with a full grin on her stunning face.

"Maggie is only five months old, so not exactly." Her face was motionless as she watched him, a caution about her he didn't understand but for some strange reason wanted to.

"It was a joke, Ms Roberts. Kids are fine."

She offered him another of her shy smiles and then dipped her head. "When can I move in?"

Mitch moved to stand beside her and noticed the scent of honeysuckle surrounded her. It was sweet and suited her and made his dick jump with interest.

"As soon as your references and DBS check come back clear." He'd actually get Will to run the check rather than the Disclosure and Barring Service who usually did the criminal records checks.

Her face dropped again, and she nodded but wouldn't meet his eyes. "Okay."

"You gonna take it?"

"Yeah, I think I am."

Mitch grinned at her, shoving his hands in his pockets to keep from the acting on the sudden urge to reach for her.

He had the distinct impression that Ms Roberts was going to make his life very interesting.

For the first time in a long time, he was excited by a woman. Whether that was a good or a bad thing was anyone's guess.

Chapter Two

Mitch pored over the blueprints for one of the proposed stops on the tour the Palace had planned for next year, trying not to pull his hair out at the number of headaches it posed from a security point of view. He looked up as Will walked inside, the new tattoo on his arm on full display.

"Aubrey know you got that?" Mitch's eyes crinkled in a grin as he nodded at the new ink covered in cling wrap.

"She does actually, she helped me choose it."

Mitch's lips turned down at the corners as he nodded. "How's her new job going?"

Aubrey had just been promoted to Lead Detective after her boss and their friend, Henry English up and fell in love with a woman who lived in Texas, forcing him to up sticks and move.

"Good. She loves it and not having to worry about Madison is a help."

"Yeah, I saw her in the conference room sorting through Jack's paperwork. Have to say if she can figure that shit out, she may be on to something."

"Pax is coming over later to give her some tips."

"Pax is the shit."

"Yeah, she is. I actually came to talk to you about your prospective tenant, though."

Mitch's antennae went up at Will's tone. "Oh?"

"Yeah, it seems Ms Roberts is in witness protection."

Mitch's eyebrows lifted, his eyes going round for a moment, but then he considered how guarded she'd been and it made a little more sense. "Does it say why?"

"I didn't dig any further. Figured that was your call. I can find out easily enough if you want."

Mitch considered it for a moment, but then something stopped him. "No, leave it for now. Whatever is in her past, she deserves a second chance. Perhaps we can give her that, plus she has a kid. If she were dangerous, they wouldn't leave a baby with her. I assume she isn't on any social services child protection list?"

Will shrugged. "Not that I could find."

"Then leave it, if she wants us to know she'll either tell us or if the need arises, we can find out."

"Fine by me. Now, I need to go see the ugly Granger of the family and tell him Mother is demanding he come for Sunday lunch."

Mitch laughed at the thought of anyone demanding Jack do anything. But then he was no different. Even at forty-five, he still jumped if his mum spoke to him in a certain voice and he never turned down her cooking. Her West Indian recipes handed down from her mother meant she was the best damn cook Mitch knew. At the thought of his mother's cooking, he figured he'd see if he had any of her jerk chicken in the freezer for later, his mouth already watering at the idea.

As Mitch drove towards his apartment, later that evening, a warm feeling settled into his belly. He'd put in a call to the letting agent telling them he was happy with the background checks—which he'd insisted on doing himself—and to let Ms Roberts know she could move in tomorrow if she liked.

Taking the stairs two at a time, he glanced at the door opposite his own and smiled. It would be nice to have someone else up here. Sure, he had Waggs and Bebe downstairs, but he liked the idea of a new face to look at and what a face it was. Maybe he'd make himself available tomorrow to help her and make sure she got moved in okay. Be a good landlord. Even as he thought it, he knew it was bullshit.

He was attracted to the beautiful woman with warm, cautious eyes and smile he knew would light up a cave if she ever let it show. With a beer in one hand and a plate of his mother's cooking in the other, Mitch flipped on the TV with a grin. Tomorrow would be a good day.

* * *

Turning to the back seat of her decrepit old Ford Focus where Maggie was shoving her entire fist in her cute but dribbly mouth, Autumn smiled. Just the feat of getting here felt like a small victory

9

in what had been fourteen months of hell. The fact the result had ended with her here, hiding, or restarting her life as a different person, alone in a town where she had nobody wasn't something she could allow herself to dwell on. If she did, she feared she might sink under the weight of it all.

No, one step at a time was her new mantra, and she and her beautiful baby girl were safe with a roof over their heads, and that was all that mattered right now. Ducking her head, she looked up at her new home. From the outside it was imposing and beautiful, a grand old Victorian home carefully restored to its original grace and grandeur. On the inside, the owner had done an excellent job of blending the old and the new.

The owner in question sprang to the forefront of her mind, making her pulse kick up as she remembered the wide smile that made his eyes twinkle, the deep baritone of his chuckle making long-forgotten body parts sit up and take notice.

Autumn pushed those thoughts away, she had no time for such things, nor indeed the trust it would take to open her heart up again and risk the devastation the last man who'd shared her bed had cost her.

"Ready to go see your new home, Roo?" Autumn asked using the nickname she'd given her baby girl, as she always seemed to settle when she was cuddled in her sling, close to her mother's body, just like a baby kangaroo.

Maggie just tried to shove her hand further in her mouth as she kicked her legs out excitedly. Autumn grinned which she found herself doing more and more since Maggie had been born, her daughter changing the course of her life and giving her more strength than someone so small should be capable of.

Getting out of the car, she bent down to lift Maggie from the car seat, lifting her to her hip as she carried the changing bag that had replaced the sleek, designer purses she used to love. With her key in hand, she walked towards the main door and opened the lock. Stepping through, she made her way to the stairs and to the third floor where she stopped.

This felt momentous, like she was finally getting a piece of her life back. Maggie grabbed a handful of her braids, attempting to shove them in her mouth. Autumn gently detangled her hair from her grasp.

"You don't want to eat that. Just wait, and as soon as I get settled in, I'll feed you. How does that sound?" Autumn often talked to Maggie like she was an adult that would answer back. It had become natural after having her as her only real company for the last few months.

Walking over the threshold of her new home, Autumn took in the space, excitement building in her chest that this was her home. Moving to the bay window, she looked down and spotted the lawned area below. Her mind instantly envisioned time spent with Maggie in the open space with the shade of the apple tree at the back.

Her daughter began to fuss, and Autumn knew if she didn't feed her child in the next few minutes all hell would break loose. Maggie went from nought to starving faster than a Bugatti Chiron on a dry track.

"Okay, Maggie, how about we feed you first?" Looking around the large space, Autumn realised she'd need to buy a few pieces of furniture. Hopefully, she could find something second-hand and then she could save some of her money for an emergency.

Plopping her butt on the ground and crossing her legs buddha style, Autumn lifted her pink tee and released the clip on her nursing bra, before Maggie latched on like the little pro she was. It was only then she realised that in her excitement she hadn't closed the door. With Maggie nursing comfortably, her little hand lying warm against her skin, the tiny snuffly noises she made showing her contentment, Autumn decided to leave it be. It was the middle of the day so everyone would probably be at work.

Her handler in the witness protection program had assured her this house and the people in it were safe for her and Maggie, but Autumn was still cautious. It would take a good while for her to trust anyone again. It didn't stop the loneliness though, or the need for human contact.

Her mind turned to thoughts of a job, and she made a mental note of how much money she had in her bank account. It would last her a few months, but she'd rather not use that unless she had too. Falling back on her editing certification and working freelance seemed the best option. Perhaps when she'd brought all her stuff in, built Maggie's cot and done a food shop, she could look into getting some work.

The door to her living room moved, and her stomach flipped with fright, her heart jumped out of her chest.

"Knock, knock?"

Mitch's head popped around the door, his twinkly brown eyes landing on first her and then Maggie before they flitted to her face again, then up to the ceiling.

"Sorry, didn't mean to interrupt. I saw your door open and wanted to check you'd gotten settled in okay."

His obvious embarrassment made her smile, as did his chivalry. "It's okay, Mitch, you can look, I'm all covered up."

Shoving his hands in his pockets, he stepped slightly into the room and dropped his eyes to her face, ensuring he didn't look lower down.

"As you can see, I've not gotten far. When this one wants feeding everything stops. She'll probably sleep afterwards though so I can bring it up then."

Mitch's eyes furrowed slightly, and he pointed behind him. "I can bring it up. Is that your Focus outside?"

Autumn nodded, her initial reaction to turn down his offer, to keep him out as she did everyone else, but he didn't give her chance.

"Is it open?"

"Well, yes, but I can manage, you don't have to."

Mitch's lips turned up at the corner, and she saw the deep dimple in his cheeky grin, her heart beating faster for a reason other than fright now. "I know, but I can get your stuff in before the removal van gets here."

Autumn blinked at him, her cheeks warming. "There isn't a moving van. I have everything I own in that car."

Mitch's handsome face turned into a frown at her words. "I see. I thought I'd said the flat isn't furnished, but maybe I didn't."

"No, you did. Furniture shopping is tomorrow's job. Today I have to get some food in. Do you know any second-hand shops around here that are good?"

"Yeah, I can hook you up."

Autumn thought she caught the slightest hint of a South London accent in his voice but wasn't sure. It made her ache for her parents and grandparents, who she missed fiercely.

Mitch disappeared from the room, and Autumn switched Maggie to the other side to feed, her baby already sleepy. A sigh of ease left her lips as she looked around her living space, it was small, but it was perfect for her and Maggie. They could build a good life here and maybe one day even make some friends.

Chapter Three

The clouds were hanging grey overhead as Autumn peered out of her window. It had been three days since she'd moved into this place, and already it was beginning to feel like home. A deep dark burgundy couch with washable covers now graced the room, along with a large cream plush area rug and a round coffee table on top.

Dark grey and white hat boxes stacked beside the couch made a cute side table, and a few plants in the window space gave it a homey feel. Maggie's room now had some homemade bunting strung around the room, and Mitch had said he could paint it if she wanted, although she liked the warm neutral colours he'd chosen. When she finally felt safe enough for her baby to go in her own room she wanted it to be perfect for her, but for now she was happy having Maggie in with her at night.

Now it was time to get out and explore the town that was her new home. Shoving her arms through a light jacket, and praying the rain stayed away, Autumn picked Maggie up from where she lay on her belly on the rug.

"Wanna go exploring, Roo?" Autumn buried her head in her baby's belly, blowing raspberries through her top and making her giggle and grab her hair.

"I'm gonna take that as a yes."

Autumn dressed Maggie in a warm coat and set her in the buggy which was waiting in the entryway. Placing the changing bag underneath, she locked her apartment and moved to the stairs. This was the bit she'd not looked forward to, carrying this heavy pram down the stairs on her own, but she'd managed so far. As she lifted it, she cursed as the metal on the wheel scraped her ankle.

"Hey, let me help you."

Autumn looked up in surprise not having heard Mitch approach behind her. He took hold of Maggie in her pram and carried her down the flight of stairs as if she weighed nothing more than a bag of sugar.

Setting her down at the bottom, he leaned in to shake her baby's hand as Maggie grinned and kicked her feet out, her big eyes twinkling at the sexy man. Even her daughter knew a fine man when

14

she saw one. And following him down the stairs had allowed her an uninterrupted view of strong shoulders and cute ass she wanted to grab hold of. Those things alone were enough, but this man was more than the sum of his cute derriere, muscles, dimples, and twinkly eyes; no, he was nice too.

"Thank you for that. I should probably try and figure that out better for next time."

"You can leave the pram under the stairs if it's easier. I originally planned it for bikes, but none of us cycle."

Autumn tipped her head. "Are you sure it won't be an imposition?"

Mitch chuckled, the deep sound humming through her. "Yes, Autumn, I'm sure it won't be an imposition."

"Hey, don't take the piss, my mama brought me up properly."

Mitch glanced her over from head to toe, and Autumn fought the desire to shiver, her body responding to this man way more than she wanted it to.

"She certainly did."

A slightly awkward silence filled with sexual tension filtered through the room, heightening her senses. Autumn had forgotten what this felt like, the giddy, heart-pounding attraction to someone that was all new.

Dropping her eyes, she blinked and garnered her nerve before locking eyes with him. "I should get going."

"I'll walk out with you." Mitch fell into step beside her, grabbing the front door and then the bottom of the pram, lifting it over the step like a pro. As they walked towards the road, she paused, wondering which way to go.

"Where ya headed?"

Mitch's easy tone was like a warm balm to her nerves. Something about it was comforting. She suspected it was because he reminded her of home and the family she missed so much.

Pushing the maudlin thoughts away, knowing they'd only harm her fragile peace, she shrugged. "Not sure yet. Me and Maggie are going exploring."

"Well, if you follow that road it leads into the main town where you'll find shops and cafés, a library, and some other stuff. If you head up the hill and then past the colleges, there's a park with a play pirate ship." Mitch looked up at the sky and Autumn followed, noting the clouds were still gathering but it wasn't as grey as before.

"I think I might have a mooch around town and check out the shops and see if there are any craft shops."

"You into all that stuff?" Mitch waved his hand in the air lamely.

Autumn grinned and shook her head at him. She mimicked waving her hand in the air. "Yes, I'm into all that stuff."

Mitch caught it and she felt the electric pull of his innocent touch all the way to her toes. "Woman, you taking the piss out of me?"

"Absolutely not."

Autumn let her hand stay in his warm and strong one, his fingers wrapping around hers lazily. They stayed in the moment, each gazing at the other as if the air around them had grown static with the pressure from their touch.

A cry from the pram broke the spell and Autumn pulled her hand away as she bent to look at Maggie. "Okay, baby girl, we'll go now." Glancing back up, she smiled shyly at Mitch. "I should go."

Mitch shoved his hands in his pockets and nodded. "Have fun."

"We will."

With a final grin for him, she and Maggie walked away. Autumn sensed the heat of his gaze on her back, and for the first time since Terrell died, she felt like a woman again. Her step brisker as if she could outrun the scary thoughts, Autumn made it into town just as the first raindrop fell.

Ducking into the cookshop, she picked up some useful kitchen utensils and a small handheld food blender that was on sale, knowing that weaning was in her not too distant future. The thought made her almost sad. Her baby was growing up too fast, and she felt cheated out of some of it by things beyond her control.

It had done one positive thing though, making her get off the hamster wheel and appreciate the moment. Instead of continually pushing herself to be the best, always working for the next promotion, she has paused. Her master's degree in chemistry had led to her dream job as a senior research chemist for one of the leading Pharmaceutical giants, but it had also been the catalyst for her downfall.

Now her life was simpler day to day. Yes, she'd made some changes, including spending the year while she was in hiding doing an online certification in editing.

Autumn had always been a geek at school, wanting to learn, feeding her brain constantly. Somehow though, she'd evaded the label of swot or teacher's pet because she got on with everyone, managing to span the divide between the cool kids and the brainiacs.

Meeting Terrell at University had only pushed her harder. Half of their relationship was based on always competing for the best grades. Landing jobs together so they could fulfil their dreams of research had been the icing on the cake.

Until it hadn't, until her tidy little world had disintegrated before her eyes, leaving her to pick up the pieces of her life and move on despite the shadow that would always linger behind her.

Walking back up the hill towards her new home, a smile filtered over her lips. It felt right being here. Somehow, she knew this had been the first excellent decision in a series of bad ones. Bumping Maggie over the doorstep, she turned to close the door and saw a stunningly beautiful woman who watched her from the doorway of the bottom flat.

With amber skin and dark brown hair with rich reds flowing through it, she was like an image from an Arabian night's novel. All she needed was the outfit, her hips were curved, waist tiny, with knowing, seductive dark eyes.

Autumn was mesmerised by her, terrifyingly so, because in those eyes she saw secrets that she'd never want to know.

"Mitch said you were beautiful, and he didn't lie."

The woman pushed off the door and stepped closer, the velour tracksuit bottoms and vest doing nothing to hide her sexuality. Autumn detected a slight accent but couldn't place it.

"Autumn, nice to meet you." Autumn moved Maggie from one hip to the other so she could offer her hand, knowing that being friendly was far less likely to arouse suspicion than being offhand.

"Bebe. It's nice to meet you, Autumn." Bebe shook Autumn's hand and then smiled as she glanced at Maggie. "She's adorable. How old?"

Autumn looked at her baby who was waving her hand around, trying to make a grab for Bebe. "Maggie is five months now."

Bebe took Maggie's tiny hand and gave it a jiggle. "You are just precious."

Her eyes found Autumn's then, and she detected a loneliness about this woman she couldn't place, a watchfulness that she saw in her own eyes as if she couldn't trust those around her or at the least, it was hard-earned.

"Would you like some help with your bags?"

Autumn looked at her feet and realised she'd bought more than she thought and would need to make two trips. "I can manage."

Bebe rolled her eyes. "I didn't ask if you could manage, I asked if you'd like help." Her otherwise scathing reply had the heat taken away by the softness of her tone.

"Thank you. That would be great."

Autumn led the way as Bebe took two of the bags and followed. Opening her flat door, she walked in and placed Maggie in her bouncer chair. Knowing she should at least offer her a drink, Autumn glanced at Bebe. "Would you like a drink?"

Bebe shook her head. "I have to get back. I have a work call coming in later. Maybe another time?"

"Sounds good."

Autumn showed her to the door, waving as she walked down the stairs. Closing it, she tipped her head at the slightly strange encounter. It was as if the other woman had been assessing her under a microscope and she wasn't sure, but she thought perhaps she'd passed some unknown test.

Mitch had said they all worked in a similar industry with odd hours, but he hadn't said what exactly, just that it involved security. Maybe that made them a suspicious bunch, but she knew no security company would get past her background checks. The witness protection people had promised her she was watertight for anyone looking into her.

Keisha Anderson no longer existed, and Autumn Roberts went back to the day of her birth, providing a full background, including speeding tickets and a credit file. With a frown she let the thought go and set about making dinner for herself. Perhaps she'd make a little extra and leave some for Mitch and Bebe. It wouldn't hurt to make friends surely, and the best way to go unnoticed according to her contact was to be ordinary and ordinary people did nice things.

Chapter Four

"I hate wearing a fucking suit." Mitch groaned as he stepped out of the back of the Range Rover outside Buckingham Palace.

Jack quirked a brow. "You can hardly come to the Palace in jeans and a fucking t-shirt."

Mitch gave a curt nod. "I know that."

One of the men they knew from previous visits walked towards them at the entrance, his hand outstretched towards Jack. He was a good guy, if a bit stiff, but as the Queen's Private Secretary, James Fitzgerald III CVO had a tough job. Mitch wondered if perhaps he knew about the traitor inside the houschold. If he did, he certainly hadn't told them who it was.

"James, good to see you."

Jack shook hands and James led them inside, his walk brisk, as if he were always on to the next thing, his mind juggling a hundred different things at once.

"Gentlemen, if you'll follow me."

Mitch walked beside Blake, taking in the surroundings of the Palace and while admiring the décor, wondered how people could live there. It was hard to conceive of this being home to anyone, but if you knew nothing else, it was a moot point.

He caught the look one of the personal protection officers sent their way as they stepped through into the Private Secretary's offices. Mitch glanced at Blake who'd also caught the barely contained look of disdain.

He understood it, they were private contractors and got paid a shit load more than the men that worked for Scotland Yard as PPOs. The fact they got paid from the Privy Purse probably pissed them off even more, but that wasn't their decision nor his. It had been the Queen's choice to have Eidolon take over certain protection roles, and Mitch had no doubt it was in no small part because of Blake.

His relationship with the Palace was a good one, and the fact that the Deputy Commissioner had shaken up the protection schedule for the Royals was the reason the Queen had taken back some control of her family's safety by employing them.

Closing the door on a large office with an antique desk, James sat. The room was impressive, but as the most influential member of the Royal household, it was to be expected. This man ran the Royal family and had access to everything. Again, the thought filtered through his mind that perhaps James would be ideally situated to set them up for a fall, but why? That was the thing he couldn't place and the reason during discussions within the team, he'd been ruled out time and again.

"I don't have a lot of time, but I wanted to give you the heads up. There's increasing tension about Eidolon having the contract for the tour next year, and we're getting pushback from Scotland Yard."

Mitch pursed his lips to stop himself from saying what he was thinking, which was suck it up, buttercup. These men needed to get a fucking grip. If they didn't like the jobs they did or the pay they got, they needed to do something about it, not sulk like kids.

"That doesn't bother us." Jack looked calm, but Mitch knew him, and he was pissed off.

"Here are the confirmed destinations for the trip." James handed Jack a sealed envelope. "And a proposed timeline."

Jack took them and placed them in his inside pocket. The next twenty minutes, the four men went over some of the pitfalls they'd already identified while James made a note of them.

James Fitzgerald was in his early fifties, slim, with blonde hair fading to grey around the temples. He'd been with the Palace for almost twenty-five years, had worked his way up so he knew it better than anyone.

Mitch, Blake, and Jack had talked about asking him if he'd heard any rumblings about them having the contract, but as he'd already come out and said there were issues being raised , there was no need.

"If that's everything, we'll head out. I'll be in touch next week about this and if that other job comes up, let me know."

"Yes, I will." James stood as did they, pausing by the door. "Jack, could I have a moment of your time in private?"

Jack looked at them and back to James. "Sure."

Mitch and Blake waited outside the door as it closed tightly behind them.

Mitch looked at Blake who shrugged. "He'll tell us if it's necessary."

Mitch watched the comings and goings of the Palace and wondered if Autumn would enjoy it or if she'd ever been. He'd found himself thinking about her a lot in the last few days, ever since their encounter on the day she'd moved in.

Mitch had seen plenty of beautiful women in his years but seeing her sitting crossed-legged on the floor of her empty flat, feeding her baby as she smiled down at her with so much love, had affected him in ways he hadn't expected. He couldn't remember seeing something so beautiful; she'd looked almost ethereal, angelic.

The tension between them when he touched her hand so innocently while helping her with the pram had been fucking electric, making his cock spring to life, his belly tightening with the need to see if she tasted as good as she looked. He'd held back though, the wariness in her eyes telling him of a past that still haunted her.

It made him want to know what had put that look there, but he wanted her to tell him, to trust him. It was a strange feeling to have about a woman he hardly knew and especially one a decade younger than him with a new baby.

The door abruptly opening behind him had him glancing back to see Jack, with a furious look on his face, marching towards them. James followed, closing the door as he stepped through and led them back to the exit.

"Safe trip back, Gentlemen." With a nod, James left.

Silence and tension swirled around Jack like a volcano about to blow. They climbed back in the car and drove towards the exit at the front of the Palace. The Range Rover had tinted windows so their coming and going wouldn't be caught on camera. And even inside the Palace, they weren't actually known to anyone other than James and the Royal family, as either Eidolon or by their real names. Secrecy was crucial to their work, so the people who were currently hating on them thought they were just a bunch of hired muscle.

"You wanna share what's on your mind?" Mitch asked as Jack took a corner dangerously fast as they exited the motorway two hours later.

Jack glanced at Blake, and Mitch watched Jack's jaw tick with anger. "Commissioner Wells has cancer. Deputy Commissioner Osbourne is running the show, and Fitz says he's changed up the PPO rotation so that he has certain men on individual Royals."

Blake frowned, his whole face going dark. "That makes no sense. The reason I left the service was that he changed it from that."

Jack nodded. "Fitz says the PPOs they have are good, but the family is unhappy with it. I got the impression that the men Osbourne is using are hand-picked by him."

Mitch sat forward. "It stinks of nepotism."

Blake turned to him. "Osbourne has always been a self-serving twat."

"You still got friends at the Yard, right?" Jack locked eyes with Mitch as he continued to drive.

"Yeah a few. Want me to make some enquiries about the guys he has on duty at the Palace?"

"Yes. I'll have Will get you the names."

"Sure. Brant wants a favour from me, so this might be a perfect time."

"Perfect. We need to see if this plays into the threat to Eidolon. I'll call a meeting tomorrow, and we can talk through what we know before I meet with Gunner later this week."

"What happened to the last meeting? Why did he cancel?"

Jack shook his head. "Don't know but you can bet I'll be finding out."

An hour later they pulled into Eidolon, and Jack stalked towards his office, closing his door.

"What the fuck happened?" Alex asked, stepping from his own office, brushing a hand through his hair as his eyebrows rose.

"Osbourne happened," Blake said and walked towards the gym.

"The Deputy Commissioner?" Alex furrowed his brow as he crossed his arms and looked at Mitch.

"Yeah, seems he's putting his own men in position at the Palace."

"Prick. I always hated him. Jack think it's anything to do with us?"

Mitch shrugged as he put his hands in the pockets of his suit trousers. "It's certainly possible. I think he wants a meeting tomorrow, but maybe you should speak to him about it."

Alex pushed up off the doorjamb. "Will do."

Mitch liked the dynamic between Alex and Jack. As second, Alex was the perfect balance to Jack, especially in situations like this, and since reuniting with Evelyn, he was even calmer than before.

Knowing that whatever was about to go down in the coming weeks wasn't going to be good news, Mitch went to grab a coffee from the kitchen before he put in a call to Brant. The man was looking to slow down, and he'd asked Mitch to put in a word with Aubrey about the detective's position that had opened up.

Mitch had been surprised at first, the guy was only thirty-nine, but then the quiet life suited some better than others. He certainly liked the pace of life here, but he still had the adrenalin rush with his job.

Entering the large kitchen, he could smell the pot of curry on the stove that Alex had made. Having a chef on the team sure made long days a hell of a lot easier. He was surprised to see Madison, having forgotten she worked there now.

"Hey, Madison, how you settling in?"

The woman looked up; her pretty face angled to him as she smiled. She looked so much like her sister, warm umber brown skin, dark chestnut coloured eyes but where Aubrey was more athletic, Madison had all the curves. In personality, the sisters were like chalk and cheese. Madison was the tornado that struck quickly, making everything fun and leaving devastation in her wake, while Aubrey was the calm aftermath.

Mitch knew she was ten years younger than Autumn, but it was more than that, the two women were poles apart. Autumn held a sadness about her, older than her years as if life had made her grow up far faster than it should have. It made Mitch want to protect her, make her smile, and ease the pain he saw in her eyes when she forgot to hide it from him.

"I'm settling okay. Lots to learn, but I want to make this work for Aubrey. It's the least I owe her after everything I put her through."

Mitch poured the dark, fragrant coffee into his mug. "You don't want this for you?"

Holding the mug up, he crossed his arm over his chest and took a sip as Madison looked at him with confusion.

"What?"

"You said this is for Aubrey. Don't you want this job?"

Madison shook her head, her eyes dropping. "I do, yes."

"But?"

"I guess life doesn't always turn out how you want it to. I wanted to be a nurse when I was younger, but then I kind of went off the rails."

"Kind of?" Mitch asked with a grin to take the sting from his words.

"No, I definitely went off the rails." She smiled back, and Mitch realised that Madison was lost. Trying to do the right thing and failing to find herself.

Pushing off the counter, he went to move past her and stopped to lay a hand on her shoulder. "You need to be happy, kid. Aubrey wants that for you. If nursing is your dream, make it happen."

With that, he walked towards the bank of offices he shared with the rest of the team and plopped himself in his chair. He was tired after an early start and not much sleep, thoughts of his sexy tenant keeping him awake. He needed to make the call and then get home for some sleep, maybe if he were lucky he'd run into her again.

Chapter Five

Autumn looked at the clock as she paced the living room of her apartment, Maggie over her shoulder as she rubbed her little girl's back trying to comfort her. She hated to see her baby like this. Today had been her last set of baby jabs until she turned one. Normally she'd have had them by now, but with the move, Autumn was late getting them done.

Rocking her back and forth as she walked the floorboards, her lips pressed to her baby's slightly warm cheek. The teething didn't help, but Autumn had expected a slight fever and crankiness. Maggie had been the same after the first two sets of vaccinations. This time she had teething to contend with too.

"Oh, Roo, I know it hurts. Silly jabs and teeth. I wish I could take the pain away quicker. Mummy will give you some more medicine soon." Autumn glanced at the clock on the microwave and saw it was a little after two in the morning. Maggie could have some more Calpol at two-thirty—thank god.

Maggie continued to cry as if her heart would break, and Autumn felt the tears prick her own eyes with helplessness. She hated this. Typically, being alone with Maggie was fine, she kind of liked that it was her and Maggie against the world, but times like this she really missed having a second set of arms to hold her. Maggie was a relatively good baby, but when she was cranky and keeping her up all night, there was nobody to share that with.

Resentment hit her as she thought of Maggie's father. He should be here but he'd been a fool, and now his ass was dead. The man she'd loved had betrayed them, leaving her in hiding with a new baby. Not even living long enough to know she was pregnant, he'd chosen money over love, and she'd never forgive that.

Autumn stopped dead as she heard a knock at her door. Turning, she listened for a noise, her heart beating faster. Who could possibly be knocking on her door in the dead of night? Caution had her stepping closer to try and hear as the knock came again.

"Autumn, it's Mitch."

Relief washed through her at the sound of his deep voice, and she moved to the door, un-flipping the extra locks she'd had installed and pulling the door open. Autumn's gaze moved over Mitch, from his gorgeous lopsided grin to his bizarrely bare feet. He wore low slung grey sweats and a white tee and looked mighty fine in her opinion.

"Just wanted to check everything was okay. I heard Maggie crying and wanted to check on you."

She stepped back as he moved through the door and past her into the living space, which was lit by a small table lamp. Autumn followed as Maggie let out another cry. Mitch looked at Maggie with concern before his eyes went back to hers.

"I'm so sorry if we woke you."

Mitch stepped closer, his face peering at Maggie as he laid his large hand over her baby's tiny back with a gentleness she hadn't expected. "You didn't wake me. I was up working."

He glanced up, and his dark brown eyes were filled with concern. He was a man who fixed things; she knew that about him already.

"Maggie had her vaccinations today, top that with teething and she's not feeling too good." Autumn yawned and quickly moved to cover her mouth. "Sorry," she mumbled.

"Here sit down before you fall down."

Mitch eased her onto the couch before he sat beside her. Autumn felt the brush of fabric from his sweats on her bare legs. Not expecting company, she was only wearing tiny sleep shorts and a jersey camisole top. Awareness slammed through her at the muscles pressed so close to her body. Mitch was a sexy distraction, but one she couldn't afford.

His brow furrowed, and he looked physically pained to hear her baby cry. "Is there anything you can give her?"

Absurdly it was that shared experience that made her feel less alone. How sad was she that the comfort from her landlord was the only thing holding her together right now?

"She's due some Calpol in fifteen minutes." Exhaustion made her feel weepy, and she swallowed past the damned lump in her throat his words brought as she answered him.

"How about I hold her, and you go get it ready?" Mitch held out his arms and Autumn paused for a split second before leaning forward and gently handing off her daughter to Mitch, his knuckles grazing her breast and causing a shiver to cascade down her body to her pussy.

This man made her feel raw in so many areas, from her reawakened libido to the vulnerability she seemed to let show when he was around.

"Sorry."

Mitch's sheepish smile told her he knew what he'd done, the twinkle in his eyes saying he was not that sorry. Autumn raised an eyebrow but said nothing, not trusting her own voice right then.

Moving to the bathroom, she grabbed the Calpol and filled the baby dormal with the medicine. The baby dummy that administered medication had been a godsend and meant she got most of the medicine in her baby not all down her top. On her way back from the bathroom, she stopped as she heard Mitch talking to Maggie.

"Sounds like you've had a rough day, darlin'. How about we get you some of the good stuff, then you have a good sleep so your mum can get some rest? Those beautiful eyes of hers look ready to close standing up."

Autumn held a hand to her chest to stop the ache where her heart constricted. It had never dawned on her that Maggie might be missing out, but hearing him speak, listening to the one-sided nonsense conversation, opened her eyes to the fact that a child needed a father.

Sagging against the wall, she closed her heavy eyes. A child could live without two parents, they could live without any, but they didn't thrive the same in her opinion. She loved her father and knew his calm protectiveness had guided her to make good decisions that perhaps her mother's more nurturing softness wouldn't have. Doubt in her ability to do this alone was like lead on her shoulders, and for just one night, she wanted to share that load with someone.

Knowing it was a fool's dream to crave a man you shouldn't want, Autumn pushed away from the wall and moved down the hall towards a silent Maggie and Mitch. Her life had changed beyond compare the night she saw her husband murdered. Now she had to fight to stay ahead of the man who would kill her in a heartbeat, leaving her baby without a mother if he got the chance.

"Hey, I'm all set."

The sight in front of her, of Mitch cradling Maggie in his big arms, the muscle of his biceps straining against her tiny body had her yearning for something she shouldn't want. He had his phone out and was playing candy crunch as Maggie made ba-ba, ma-ma noises at him.

His head twisted to her, and he grinned a triumphant grin. "Your girl likes candy crunch, got me to level seventy-six," he looked back to Maggie, "didn't ya, bubby."

Autumn smiled as she took a seat facing Maggie and Mitch on the couch. "She likes the colours." As she spoke, she offered Maggie the dormal, and her daughter sucked it into her mouth, taking the medicine like a champ.

"She likes that."

Mitch grinned at her and Autumn allowed herself to wonder what it might be like if things were different and she wasn't living with this huge secret.

"Have you tasted the stuff? It's like liquid candyfloss. Of course she likes it."

Mitch chuckled. "Can't say as I've tasted Calpol, honey."

Honey, that one simple word meant nothing, and yet the way it made her feel was everything. She'd become invisible in the last eighteen months, even before that if she were honest with herself.

Her husband had been so engrossed with what was going on at work he hadn't been at home a lot and he'd spent every waking hour on his phone or laptop. After his death, she'd become the sole witness that could put Linton Allen inside for the rest of his life. The star witness, whose testimony was the only thing that mattered, convinced by the Crown Prosecution Service that they'd protect her until he went away for life. But he hadn't gone down, he'd walked away because of a technicality, and now she was a woman in hiding, a single mother and sole provider for her child. Yet, for one second, for a fleeting moment, she'd felt like a woman, and it was good, better than good, it made her feel alive.

"Autumn?"

She shook her head to dislodge the thoughts and her reaction to the simple word. "Yes?"

Her eyes met Mitch's, and she hid her thoughts from him. She'd been told countless times that her eyes were too expressive, but for a few moments his were too, and she saw so many questions there she couldn't answer, it hurt to look at him.

"I asked if you wanted to take her. I think she needs a change."

The information woke her up, and she leaned in to take Maggie from him as a single tear welled up in her eye. Mitch allowed her to take Maggie, who already seemed a little better, her cheeks less red.

"Hey, what's this?"

His coarse finger touched the skin of her cheek as he caught the wetness before it ran down her cheek. He was so close now she could feel his heat surrounding her. How she longed to sink into his strength, to absorb some of it so she could store it for times liked this.

It had only been two weeks since they'd met, and yet she knew she was safe with Mitch. Sure, she was attracted to him but it was more than that. Autumn felt like she knew him, deep in her soul knew they were connected in a way she couldn't understand.

Meeting his eyes, she offered him a small grin. "Just tired. I'm weepy and pathetic when I'm tired."

A big hand cupped the back of her neck, and his head dipped closer. Autumn's breath hitched, and she thought he might kiss her—wanted him to kiss her. Wanted to feel this heat, know his strength, but at the last second, he pressed his lips to her forehead.

"Crying isn't a weakness. Raising a baby alone is fucking hard work. You need to give yourself a break. You've had a shitty time of it, so go easy on yourself and let people help you."

Autumn had a second's hesitation as she wondered if he knew her secret, but that was impossible. She badly wanted to accept his offer, to let him in and lean on him. She and Bebe had forged a friendship of sorts, and that had been easy. Autumn had baked her some cupcakes to say thanks for her help and Bebe had put the kettle on so they could share them.

This was different though. She sensed that she and Mitch could be so much more. Maybe just it was the sensual bite of attraction or perhaps more, but she knew it had the ability to undo her defences in ways she wasn't sure she wanted.

"I can't be anything other than your friend, Mitch," she warned him with honesty leaking from every pore.

"Let's start there then." His grin made her think of sweaty nights and a long lazy morning, but she nodded. "But first, let's get this one changed, she's stinking up the place."

Autumn laughed at his words, forgetting that he was probably not as desensitised to her daughter's lethal behind as she was, but his words had done as she knew he'd intended and stopped her tears.

Standing, she walked towards her bedroom. Maggie was still in a cot next to the bed and her gaze dropped to the floor where her rumpled sheets lay across the air mattress she was sleeping on.

"Can you pass me the wipes?" she asked Mitch, who was looking around the room with a frown. He looked annoyed, and she wondered what had crawled up his ass. "Mitch, wipes?"

He looked up seeming perplexed. "Huh?"

"Baby wipes. This getting everywhere."

Mitch pulled a face, and she thought he was going to puke as he handed her the wipes and stepped back a pace. Autumn cleaned up her baby quickly and had her in a new onesie in minutes.

Autumn kissed Maggie's cheek. "There, all cleaned up."

Placing Maggie in her cot she gave her the pacifier and covered her with the blanket before rubbing a finger over her cheek, all the love and wonder she felt building up in her heart.

Walking out of the room behind Mitch, she pulled the door almost closed. The broad expanse of his shoulders in front of her made her body ache to touch him, her fingers almost reaching for him, only stopping herself by sheer will power.

"Why are you sleeping on a goddamn air mattress?"

Autumn was taken aback as he rounded on her, his face tight with irritation. She blinked, not expecting the question or the tone in which he'd asked it. Her own temper flared at his high handed manner, and her eyebrows rose as her hands went to her ample hips.

If it was one thing Autumn had, it was tits and ass, and she used them to her advantage now because she sure didn't have height on this man, but she could throw down attitude with the best of them. "Excuse me?"

He stepped close, and she saw the muscle twitch in his jaw as he looked down at her, his body towering over her own. "You heard me. Why the fuck are you sleeping on the floor?"

"It is not the floor, it's an air bed."

"Bullshit, it's the fucking floor. You need a real bed so you get some decent rest. No wonder you're fucking tired sleeping on that piece of shit."

"I sleep fine."

"Of course you do, honey."

The sarcasm wasn't lost on her, neither was the sweep of his eyes over her body.

"I have a baby. Tiredness is in the job description."

"Well, it won't be because you have a shit bed, not on my watch. First thing tomorrow we're going bed shopping, so be ready."

His arm banded around her and hauled her against his body as he kissed her hard. His tongue plundered her mouth as her body went slack against the onslaught of desire that had her leaning into him. As fast as it began, it was over and he pulled away, his hand still holding her hips steady as she swayed on her weak legs.

"Damn, woman, you pack a punch." Before Autumn could respond, he was at the door, regarding her with heavy-lidded eyes, his hand on the door. "Lock up."

Autumn nodded and moved to do as he said, her fingertips brushing her lips, a smile echoing over her face.

Chapter Six

Mitch lifted his hand and knocked briskly on Autumn's door before dropping his hand to his side. Last night when he'd gone over to her place he'd had no intention of kissing her, not a thought in his head about following through on his fantasies, but he'd learned so much about her in the time he'd been there. That knowledge had changed everything for him.

She was a fucking phenomenal mother—strong and fierce yet so damn sweet she made his teeth ache. Her body was sinful, and every movement she made, no matter how innocent, screamed sensuality. Autumn was sexier than any stripper could ever hope to be in those tiny cotton shorts she'd had on. Her long muscular legs ended in a curvy ass he'd wanted to grab onto with both hands while he kissed the fear from her eyes. Autumn's temper when he'd bossed her around had been to blame, he'd reasoned when he got back to his own apartment. It was that fire that tipped him over the edge so he couldn't hold back from kissing her.

Women with spirit were a personal weakness for him. He had no use for meek and mild, he didn't want a woman who'd break, he wanted a warrior and most especially when they looked like Autumn did. She was beautiful no doubt, but the way she'd looked at Maggie had awakened something Mitch hadn't known about himself. Her love for her child was primal, and he knew she'd die for Maggie in a heartbeat. It had him wanting to know her secrets, to find out what she was running from.

Mitch had been a copper a long time, it had taken him until he was almost twenty to drag himself completely away from the gang mentality he'd grown up with. Even after his mum had moved away, he'd been a pain in her ass, getting into trouble for petty crimes. Only the kindness from one detective had changed his outlook, that same man had gone on to become his step-father, and he'd always be thankful for Tony and the role he'd played in his life.

Now his role with Eidolon allowed him access to situations where people were at their most vulnerable, and he tried to do the same, to be that man for others. He'd seen the cautious look, had noticed the extra locks on the door and windows, ones he hadn't installed, and it caused questions to worm through him. Who was she running from and why?

As he'd stepped into a cold shower at four am, it had struck him that he wanted her in his bed, but he also liked her in his life. In what capacity he didn't know yet, but he intended to find out, and in the meantime, he'd do whatever he could to get her to open up so he could protect her and that began with a fucking bed.

The door swung back, and he was greeted with a small smile from Autumn, a flicker of pleasure in her eyes as they roved over him quickly. Maggie was in her arms and looking much happier than she had last night.

"Morning, honey." He stepped through as she paced into the living room, bending to grab a toy from the floor and giving him a cracking view of her ass.

She stood and spun, catching him looking, giving him a glare which lacked any heat at all. Mitch grinned back unrepentantly, lifting a brow in challenge. Him looking at her was something she'd have to get used to because he planned on doing it a lot more.

Autumn dropped her gaze first as he'd known she would, and he tucked his hands in his pockets as he took in the shadows under her beautiful, expressive eyes.

"This isn't necessary, you know. I'm sure you have much better things to do than take me bed shopping."

Mitch crossed his arms. "Nope."

Autumn huffed, shaking her head, and turned, thrusting Maggie at him. Mitch automatically took her, bringing Maggie to his chest as Autumn left the room. He'd literally been left holding the baby. His eyes lowered to the child who was looking at him as she babbled nonsense words. Her little arms were waving wildly before she smacked him in the face with a wet, slobbery hand.

"Hey, hold up, champ." He took her delicate hand in his as she wrapped her fingers around his thumb and tried to shove it in her mouth. "You don't want to be doing that, gorgeous." He chuckled as he resisted and distracted her by tickling her belly.

"Here, try this." Autumn walked from the bedroom wearing a denim jacket over a burgundy maxi dress and converse trainers, passing him a coloured set of plastic shapes. He handed them to Maggie, who took them and shook them wildly before gnawing on them.

"Thanks, thought I might lose a digit for a sec there."

Autumn was standing beside him, and he looked down at her as her scent enveloped him. He'd been able to smell her scent all night and to say it was distracting was an understatement, and yet he wanted more.

"You ready to go?"

Mitch nodded. "If you are."

Autumn took Maggie from him, grabbing her large changing bag, keys, phone, and wallet. He watched her check the locks on the windows before she followed him to the door, locking up and double-checking it was secure.

She offered him a self-conscious grin. "Sorry, I'm a little OCD about safety."

Mitch tipped his head, pursing his lips. "That's a good thing. I'm the same myself."

"You are?" Taking the pram from under the stairs, Mitch lifted it and folded it flat.

"I am. Being in the force and seeing the things I have makes you extra cautious. We're taking my car." He nodded at the pram as she watched him.

"Oh, I don't have a rain cover and it looks like the weather could turn."

He saw the flicker of disappointment cross her face before she hid it, the look gave him hope and almost made him smile, but he fought it.

"No problem, I already borrowed one until you can sort one out."

"How? When?"

"My friend Nate lives a few doors down. His little girl Nancy isn't using this one and we can use it until you get your own."

Autumn gave him a suspicious look. "How did you know my rain cover got ripped?"

Mitch shrugged. "I didn't. I just saw you didn't have one on the pram and when I was talking to Nate, saw they did so I asked to borrow it."

"Why?"

"I didn't want to give you an excuse to say no." He looked a little sheepish then and she wanted to smile but forced it back.

"Oh, okay."

34

Mitch took her elbow, leading her to his car before opening the back door.

"Wow, you fitted the car seat too. When did you do that?"

Mitch could have lied and basked in her praise but came clean. "Your car was open, and we'll talk about that at some point." He scratched his chin, biting his tongue from lecturing her about her disregard to her safety with everything going on. "Anyway, Nate fitted it for me. This baby paraphernalia is a fucking nightmare to figure out. I honestly don't know how you make it look so easy."

Autumn laughed, and the sound made the hair on his nape prickle with unexpected joy and desire. It was a rich, warm sound that came from deep in her belly, causing his dick to jump to attention. Mitch wanted to taste her lips as she bent, utterly unaware of the effect she had on him, and buckled Maggie in the car seat.

He bit back the groan as her ass brushed his leg and had to step back, or he'd end up getting arrested or slapped. Choosing the safe option, he moved to the driver's side and got in. Autumn followed suit, a wide grin on her face as she buckled in and turned to look at Maggie.

"She loves the car. She looks so happy."

Mitch wasn't looking at Maggie; his eyes were drawn to the lightness in her voice, the crinkle at her eyes as her smile went wide and unguarded. She was so beautiful when she let herself relax. Autumn was beautiful all the time but unreserved she was a goddess. He'd been on this earth for forty-five years and not once had a woman affected him like this. He'd had women, lots of them, some had even been serious, but none had made him feel this terrifying desperation like Autumn did.

As he drove towards the furniture store, he tried to sort his thoughts into something that made sense. He'd watched as his teammates fell in love—Alex and Evelyn, Blake and Pax. He'd been a witness as Reid succumbed to Callie, had laughed when Liam fell for the Princess and been happy for every single one of them. But he hadn't quite understood the dynamic of it. The attraction he got, but not what made one person know without any doubt that they would die for another, that their life would be forever changed if that person was no longer with them.

Now he felt a semblance of understanding because he had the sneaky suspicion it was happening to him. Pulling into the car park,

35

he helped Autumn put Maggie in the pram, and walked beside her as they browsed the store. He happily walked beside them as Autumn looked around, admiring the different collections before they got to the bedroom section.

"Well, what is it you want?" Autumn swept a hand at the different beds in front of them. Wooden and metal frames, divans, even one with a spot for a TV in it.

Mitch tipped his head to her. "Which do you like?"

Autumn gave it some thought before she moved to sit on one of the divans. It was a double in the lower price range. "This one works. It has storage and the price is good."

Mitch had got what he needed from that and made a decision. Autumn wanted storage and she'd get it but not with a cheap, shitty bed and certainly not a double. If he had his way, he'd be sharing that bed with her, and he needed a king size.

Twenty minutes later they were back in the car.

"You didn't need to buy the most expensive bed, Mitch."

He glanced at her, his eyebrow raised. "No, but I wanted too."

"Thank you. It was kind."

"Not kind, honey. If I have my way, we'll be sharing it before long." He knew honesty was the best option for this woman. To be anything less would make her feel cheated or conned, and he didn't want that.

Her mouth dropped open in an O. "Do you always just tell it like it is?"

Mitch shrugged. "What's the point in hiding it. I like you, Autumn. I want you in my bed."

"And what if I don't want that?" Her voice had lost the teasing tone, and he heard the wariness creep in as they pulled into the drive at home.

Switching off the engine, he unbuckled and twisted to her, noting the vulnerability in her pretty brown eyes. "Autumn, I like you. You're fun, sexy, cute and I'm drawn to you like I've never been to anyone before, but if you don't want that, then nothing happens. You carry on being my tenant and I continue to be your landlord and maybe your friend if you'll let me." Mitch took her hand, rubbing the silky soft skin with his thumb. "But I think you like me too."

"I do, but I have so much baggage, Mitch. I'm not sure I can offer you anything other than friendship, and not because I don't want to, I do. I feel this connection too, but you don't know me, and I can't share some things with you and I may never be able to."

He took her warning, trying to decide if he should tell her he knew about the witness protection and knowing she'd never forgive him for lying to her. "Let's go inside and finish this conversation." Without waiting, he got out of the car and crossed to get Maggie as Autumn sat seemingly shocked at his sudden change.

When they got inside, he moved straight towards her apartment, waiting at the door as she unlocked it. Autumn shed her jacket, dropping it on the arm of the chair as she took Maggie and laid her on her mat.

Mitch took a seat and patted the chair. "Come here, Autumn." He watched her pace for a minute before she sat beside him, her hands in her lap. "I know you're in witness protection."

He heard her indrawn breath and grasped her hand as he saw her pulse begin to hammer in her neck, the blood leaving her face.

"How?"

"The company I work for isn't your average security company. We have access to data that most don't. They ran your background check and Will, our boss stroke tech guru, told me."

"I'm going to be sick."

She rushed to her feet and was running to the bathroom before he could stop her. He followed her to the bathroom and saw her on her knees over the toilet bowl. Crouching, he took her braids in his hand, holding them away from her face. He felt terrible to have done this to her, but he knew the cost of lies and deception. Look at what it had done to Gunner. His brow tightened at the thought of his former teammate.

Autumn stood and turned to the sink. "Give me a sec."

She waved him off, and he moved back into the living room to see Maggie playing happily on the floor with her mobile over her head. She really was a good baby. Without the pram, it would've been difficult to know she was there today.

He watched as Autumn's eyes flickered to him before she looked away when she entered the lounge. Moving past him she went to the kitchen and put the counter between them. He guessed it was her way of putting up a mental barrier. He knew she wasn't scared of him, or she wouldn't leave her baby on the floor near him.

37

Autumn Roberts gave away far more than she realised, her guard having lowered around him the last couple of weeks.

"I don't know the details, Autumn, but we needed to know who'd be living here because of the jobs we do. I want you to share with me what happened if and when you're ready, but it makes no difference to the way I feel."

"You can't say that. The people who want me dead are dangerous. They could hurt you if we got involved. It's bad enough knowing I brought Maggie into this nightmare but you too, I can't."

Mitch crossed the space quickly, moving close so he could touch her. His hands reached for her arms, and he felt her shiver. "I'm dangerous, Autumn. My friends are all lethal. If anyone can keep you safe, it's us. Tell me or don't, but whatever you do, don't make the decision for me."

"I'm scared."

He pulled her shaking body to his chest then and held her tight, wanting her to feel safe in his arms. He knew he'd just lied to her. He did want to know, he was desperate to find out so he knew what they might face, but he also wanted her to trust him enough to share it. "I know, honey. Let me help you."

Autumn tipped her head up to look at him through eyes wet with tears. "What if I can't talk about it? Every time I think I'm free it drags me back under. I'm not sure I can open that wound again."

"Then we deal. I like you for who you are now. I want the future, not the past."

"I can't promise you that."

"Then give me the now."

He swept her hair back from her face giving her time to answer. He saw the war playing out in her head as she wore her emotions on her face for him.

"I'd like that."

"Good. Now can I kiss you?" At that moment, Maggie let out a wail and Autumn smirked as he groaned. "Guess not."

Mitch let her go, feeling lighter than he had in ages.

Chapter Seven

Hitting send on the uploaded manuscript, Autumn leaned back with a relieved sigh. That was the last of the editing done for the one and only job she'd managed to get this week, but it paid well enough, and everyone had to start somewhere. Rubbing her aching neck from hours bent over a laptop, she stood and walked to the window. It was a beautiful sunny day in May, and she wanted to spend the afternoon in the garden with Maggie.

Like her, Maggie loved the fresh air, and she had some borders to plant thanks to Mitch allowing her to treat the garden as her own. Pouring a glass of water, she took a sip as she considered the last three weeks. He'd shocked her with his revelation, but after she'd gotten over the surprise and fear, it had been a relief.

Hiding was hard work, especially for someone like her who was open and expressed her feelings on her face. Autumn was reassured that she was safe with Mitch after putting in a call to her contact at the National Crime Agency. Having been in Hereford five weeks now she'd spoken with the person on the local force who'd be her new protection point of contact, and they were happy with her set up and entirely up to date on her case.

Her frustration though was with Mitch, and how slow he was taking things. He'd kissed her, but that was it, and she'd wondered if perhaps he was worried about her being a widow and still mourning her husband. He couldn't be more wrong, her love for Terrell had died the night she'd found out about his illegal activities, although their problems had begun a long time before that.

A cry from the monitor had her setting her glass down with a smile and turning to get Maggie from her bed. The past was where it belonged, and now she had to concentrate on her and her daughter's future.

A short time later with a blanket lying on the grass, Autumn was planting a shrubbery border along the lawn that would offer colour almost year-round. Mitch had told her gardening wasn't his thing and said she could do whatever she liked with it. He'd drawn the line at letting her pay for it though, and they'd argued about that until he'd kissed her, and she'd forgotten everything but the taste of him.

The man could kiss like the very devil until her brain was mush and her body was screaming for more.

With the sun warm on her back, it was hard not to be happy, the smile pulling at her lips felt rusty as if it had been too long since she'd really smiled, but she was optimistic, cautiously so, but she felt hope for the first time in a long while. Where things might go with her sexy landlord she had no idea, but she was enjoying being with him and the easy friendship they'd developed to go with whatever else was happening between them. If it turned out to be just friendship then so be it, although she knew it would be mind-blowing to have sex with a man like Mitch. Something told her he'd know exactly how to find the places on her body that made her moan with pleasure.

Autumn glanced up as the man in question ambled towards her, his easy stride long and loose and at odds with the coiled power in him that never seemed to leave. Even when they were alone she sensed it.

"Hey, want some help?"

Autumn looked up at him from under her hand, as she shielded her eyes from the afternoon sun. "I thought you hated gardening."

Mitch crouched so that she could see him without the sun at his back, his face inches from hers. "I do, but I like being around you."

Autumn smiled, her heart warming at his words. "Were you always such a charmer?"

Mitch gave her a lopsided grin as he winked. "From the day I was born."

"Arrogant."

His face moved in closer, the look in his eye devilish, making her feel almost dizzy with desire for him.

"Is it arrogant if it's true?"

She grasped his dark green tee with a muddy hand and pulled his lips closer. "Yes, but apparently I like it."

He smiled against her lips before kissing, her softly. It was languorous and lazy, just like the early summer day stretching before her. A moan of pleasure slipped past her lips as he kissed his way towards the pulse at her neck.

"Fucking perfect."

Mitch pulled back, and she swayed, dazed by the feeling he evoked in her.

Leaving her, Mitch fell to his knees beside her daughter, who was now having fun rolling onto her back. Her little hands came up, a smile on her face as she tried to grab for Mitch.

"Hello, gorgeous, how are you today?"

Autumn loved the way he included her baby in every interaction; he'd even changed a diaper, albeit reluctantly and with gagging noises.

"How come you call her gorgeous and me honey?"

Mitch glanced at her as he played bicycle with her daughter's legs making her belly laugh. He cocked his head, squinting against the sun. "She's gorgeous and you, well, you smell like honeysuckle. Every time I think of you, the scent comes to mind."

Autumn loved that he thought of her enough to give her a nickname, knew she was growing more and more attached to this man.

"I like that," she said simply.

"So, tell me what to do?"

He grabbed a trowel and held it aloft like a weapon as she showed him how to dig a trough for her to plant the small shrubs. Autumn could so easily imagine him as law enforcement. He'd told her he'd worked for SO19 as a sniper and now his job was as the weapons expert at the company where he worked. He hadn't told her much else, just that they did a little of this and that for the government.

Autumn had tried to guess when she was alone with her thoughts, but too often her imaginings ended up like a blockbuster movie, with espionage, black ops, and government cover-ups, so she'd given up. Her mum had always told her that her wild imagination would get her into trouble. How ironic was it that it was the safe job, the steady husband, that had been her downfall.

"What's wrong?"

Autumn jumped at Mitch's voice so close and twisted to find him sitting beside her, his worried gaze on her face. She didn't want to lie to him, but she didn't know how much she should tell him either. She shrugged. "Just thinking about my family."

His hand came up to tug her across him, her ass in his lap as he bandied his arms around her. "You miss them."

It was a statement rather than a question, but she nodded anyway. "I do. We were always close, especially me and my

41

younger brother. He was ten years younger than me. My mum had me when she was fifteen, so we were close too, even though we were totally different." She stopped, not sure what else she could reveal without breaking the rules.

"How about you tell me about them without telling me any identifiers? That way you won't break any rules."

Autumn angled her head to look up at him. His dark eyes were alight with understanding, even as his brows pinched in a frown. Reaching up, she smoothed the offending frown before stroking her hand down his stubbly cheek. "How do you always know what I'm thinking?"

It was something she'd wondered before. He often anticipated what she might say or do, and it was a little unsettling to know he knew her so well, and yet he didn't know her past.

Mitch pressed a kiss to her temple, before resting his cheek against her head. "Fuck if I know, Autumn, but from the second I laid eyes on you something happened here." He rubbed his hand over his chest, brushing against her arm. "I've seen it happen to others, but I've never had this kind of thing happen to me. I feel as if I know you deep in my soul, as if I can anticipate your thoughts. Does that sound weird?"

Autumn shook her head. "No, I feel it too, this comfort with a person that's so natural it's as if you've known them your whole life. I felt it the first time I held Maggie. Like she'd always been part of my life, and yet it was all so new."

They were silent for a few moments until Maggie drew their attention away with her cries.

"She needs feeding." Autumn lifted Maggie and quickly settled herself on the warm grass, lifted her shirt discreetly, and let her daughter feed. Mitch was sitting with his long legs in front of him, body braced on his arms behind him, watching her.

She wriggled self-consciously. "What?"

"Nothing really, I've just never realised the beauty of a feeding mother until you. It's so calming to witness the pure love between a mother and her child."

"It is, and it's not something you can ever explain until you become a parent, but it's fierce the love you have for them. There's nothing I wouldn't do for her, not a single thing on this planet. She's the only person I've felt that with." Autumn knew she was revealing more than perhaps she should but couldn't stop the honesty.

"What about her father?"

Autumn looked away at the question, knowing it was so complicated, almost impossible to pick apart but wanting to tell Mitch the truth. "We met in college, got together almost straight away. We became study partners and fell in love. Got jobs together and then got married. It was perfect, we were perfect."

Autumn sighed. "Or at least I thought we were and then cracks started to show. He was staying out later, making calls late at night. I thought he was having an affair and confronted him."

Autumn went to say his name and bit it back. "He was absolutely adamant he wasn't and assured me it was work, even showed me the call log to the office. I believed him, and we started trying for a baby." Autumn glanced down at Maggie and couldn't regret that part in the slightest.

"Things were great, and then I found several discrepancies at work. I can't explain more without giving you the details, but I discovered he was breaking the law in a big way. I confronted him, and he broke down and told me he was in deep and it was too late to back out. I begged him to run away with me, but I think secretly he'd grown to love the power he had and the cash, and ultimately, he chose that over me."

"His loss."

Autumn stared into space, lost in her memories of that time. Every time she let her mind go there it hurt, but today with Mitch beside her, it hurt less. "Yes, and now he's dead, so it makes no difference. He can't hurt us now."

Mitch didn't fish for more details, and she was grateful for that, knowing she didn't have the energy to fight him after opening up like that.

"Wanna grab an ice cream?" Mitch's eyes twinkled as he leaned forward and kissed her neck. "Or do you want to make out?"

"Can't we do both?"

"Fucking hell." His deep voice rumbled against her sensitive skin, and she shivered.

As they drove towards the 'world's best ice cream shop' according to Mitch, the window open and the cool air brushing her skin, she smiled. Her life was good, better than good, it was great. A lovely home, a man who she was really beginning to care about by her side, who treated her and Maggie like gold, and more importantly she was safe. It was a thought that would bite her on her ass just seconds later when her phone rang, and her world rocked again.

Chapter Eight

"Hello?"

Mitch twisted his head as Autumn answered her phone, curious by the surprised tone of her voice. Few people should have her number so any calls should be at least half expected. He glanced back at the road, slowing, and pulling into a layby seeing the expression on her face. Her eyes shot to his, wide and horrified, with fear in their depths that ripped his guts open like a blunt knife.

"How did you get this number?" Her voice was barely a whisper as her fingers gripped the handset, going bloodless. Her breath was coming faster, as she began to panic.

Mitch had seen enough. Taking the phone from her, he snarled, "Who is this?" He could hear the person breathing on the other end of the phone, and then it went dead.

Hanging up he placed the phone in the centre console having no intention of giving her the phone back before Will could get a look at it.

"Who was that?"

His voice was sharper than he intended, concern making him react and take charge as if this was a mission. He saw her flinch and softened his tone as he slipped his seat belt off, and doing the same to hers, dragged her into his arms. Her body was shaking so badly it felt as if she was having a seizure, her breath see-sawing in and out rapidly as she descended into a panic attack.

"Just breathe slowly, in and out. Count with me, honey. One. Two. Three in. Four. Five. Six out." He did it with her hoping she'd mimic his actions and was glad when her breathing evened out.

"Talk to me, honey. Who called you?"

"My brother-in-law."

Mitch frowned, knowing he wasn't getting all the information and trying to remain calm and give her what she needed emotionally. "Okay?"

Her shaking began to subside, and she pulled away, her defeated eyes making him want to tear the person who'd put that look there apart.

45

"He was the man who got my husband involved with the person who killed him, and who I'm running from."

Mitch didn't like it. Nobody should be able to get hold of her and certainly nobody involved with her case. "What did he say?"

"That he needed to speak to me."

"Is this your sister's husband or your husband's family?" His brain was running through scenarios in his head as she spoke.

"It's my husband's family, his sister's husband."

"And he was the middle-man between your old man and this person?" He didn't like to think of this unknown man as Autumn's husband.

"Yes."

Mitch took her hand and made sure her eyes were on him before he spoke. The look of trust she put in him was overwhelming, and he knew he wouldn't do anything to make her regret that.

"Honey, I think we should bring my team in on this. We have the resources to protect you properly and the manpower. But to do that you need to tell us everything." Her back stiffened as she tried to pull away, but he held fast.

"Autumn, this man found you, so it stands to reason the man he works for can as well." He saw the flair of fear mist her eyes, her jaw flexing as she swallowed. "I'm not trying to frighten you, but you need to see the bigger picture here."

"But I'm not meant to break the terms of my protection. They could take even that away, and then Maggie and I will be on our own. Believe me, I don't want to be in this position. I trust the police to keep me safe only marginally more than I trust the man that ruined my life." Autumn pushed her hair out of her way in a nervous gesture he'd seen her do before.

Mitch wondered at her comment, knowing many people were wary of the police force, but not pegging Autumn as one. "They won't. Trust me when I say we have the contacts to stop that happening. We're also a fuck of a lot more trained for this than the local police force, and that's taking nothing away from them. Fuck, our boss's fiancée, Aubrey, is a detective on the force."

"Aubrey?" Autumn tipped her head at his words, her brown furrowing.

"Yeah, Aubrey Herbert. She's a good friend."

"She's my contact. She seemed okay, actually."

"Then this is perfect. Aubrey will vouch for us and make sure you don't lose police protection. She's one of the good ones, Autumn. But, honey, whatever happens, you're not alone. You and Maggie have me, and I have my team."

He saw her shoulders sag and couldn't resist pulling her into his arms, wanting to keep her there until any threat against her was taken care of permanently.

"What if I put you in danger?"

Mitch smothered the chuckle at her words, knowing she could have no idea his life was in danger every time he took a job protecting the Royal family, chasing down terrorists in Iran, or removing rebel dictators from power. It was all a risk and yet holding her, he recognised this would be a bigger risk for him and not because he could get hurt, but because she and Maggie could. "Don't worry about me. Just let me do this for you, Autumn. Please."

Her body relaxed just a fraction, and he knew she was relenting.

"Fine, but I want to be there when you ask your boss. I don't want you getting fired for me."

Mitch let his grin show as he pulled back. Looking into her beautiful upturned face, he wrapped a hand lightly around her braids and pulled, tipping her head back. He saw the heat burn through her eyes, as her breathing changed, the pulse in her neck pounding wildly. He wanted her so badly it hurt.

He'd taken more cold showers in the last three weeks than he'd had his entire adult life. This woman had him feeling like a teenager again, his cock pulsed with the desire to feel her heat gripping him as she rode him, her head thrown back like the queen she was.

"Love that you want to protect me, honey. Makes me so fucking hard that my woman wants to stand beside me. Have a mind to lay you back in this seat and taste every inch of your body, to show my gratitude, but much as it kills me to say it, we can't."

Her tongue moved to wet her lips as her chest heaved, her breathing accelerating to match her pulse. "Mitch." Her voice was a plea, one he'd move heaven and earth to grant but not now.

"Wish I could give you what your eyes are begging me for, honey, but when I make you mine, I want to know it's in a bed, where I can take my time."

"Okay."

He loved how her eyes were almost black, her voice raspy with desire. Mitch bent and took her mouth, kissing her with the promise of so much more, his tongue tasting her sweetness. Pulling back, he grinned as she swayed towards him loving that she reacted as she did, with total abandon.

"Let's go see my boss."

He clipped her seat belt back on before doing the same with his own. He kept her hand in his as he turned the car around, before laying it on his thigh, his hand on top of hers as he drove towards Eidolon. It was time for the truth to come out and for him to get rid of the threat hanging over her pretty head for good.

Autumn shot him a shy smile, and he lifted her hand to his lips, brushing a kiss over her delicate skin.

"It will be okay, Autumn, I promise. I won't let anyone hurt you or Maggie."

"I thought this would all be over by now."

"How so?"

"The man who is after me should be in prison. The CPS convinced me that if I testified, they had a watertight case against him. Then my life would be my own again while he served life in prison."

He glanced at her as he slowed for the traffic lights wondering what had gone wrong within the Crown Prosecution Service. "What happened?"

Autumn sighed deeply. "He got off on a technicality. Someone had signed the gun used to kill my husband out of evidence without authorisation, and the case fell apart."

"Wow, no wonder you don't trust the police to keep you safe."

Autumn pursed her lips. "Until you, I didn't trust anyone, thought I never would again. Something about this town makes me want to see a way out for us." She glanced back at a sleeping Maggie, and he followed her eyes in the rearview mirror. The peace on her innocent face making him ache for the position she and her mother found themselves in.

"The men I work with are good people, and so are their girlfriends," Mitch reassured her, but she said nothing, seemingly lost in her head. Not wanting to push, he just held her hand on his thigh as he drove.

Arriving at Eidolon, he pulled up at the gate and greeted Frank with a wave, who let them through. The man was old school, a former General and his friend Zack Cunningham's father-in-law. Retirement hadn't suited Frank, so Jack had offered him this job part-time and he took it very seriously, which was good because the threat level against them was increasing.

Mitch glanced at Autumn, her wide eyes were on the building, and he could feel her trepidation. "Ready?"

She controlled a sigh blowing air through pursed lips. "As I'll ever be."

Mitch nodded as he helped her unstrap the car seat, a still sleeping Maggie inside. With Maggie in one hand, he took hold of Autumn's in the other and led her inside. Stopping at the retina scanner, he let the machine do its thing before pushing through the door.

He glanced at the front area where Madison should be and saw it was empty. Following the sounds of men's voices, he moved down the hallway towards the conference room. Jack and Alex glanced up from where they were looking through aerial photographs as he walked in, both their brows raising slightly as they looked behind him where Autumn was hanging back.

"I need your help," he stated, and Alex stood as Jack surveyed Mitch without any sign of what he was thinking on his face.

Alex walked to Autumn and reached his hand out. "Alex Martinez. Pleased to meet you. You must be Autumn, right?"

Mitch could have kissed him for making Autumn feel instantly more relaxed, so much that he felt the tension leak out through the hand he held in his own.

"Yes. Nice to meet you, Alex."

Mitch led her to a seat across from Jack and Alex as Jack removed the pictures from the table. Setting Maggie down at her feet, he took the seat beside her as Alex returned to his chair.

"What do you need?" Jack asked the question, and Mitch's shoulders relaxed.

He'd known his team would help them out but hearing it was still a good thing.

"I'm in the witness protection program, and I think the people I'm hiding from have found me."

49

Jack betrayed not a second of surprise, and Mitch knew then that he already knew she was in the program, most likely from Will.

"How do you know these people found you?" Alex sat back in his chair, his ankle crossed over his knee. He looked chill, but Mitch knew he wasn't.

"We were in the car when Autumn got a call from her brother-in-law. He's the one who acted as a middle-man between the people she testified against and her husband, who they murdered." Mitch saw a flicker of emotion as Jack clenched his jaw, his eyes dropping to Maggie who was stirring.

Autumn quickly bent to lift her daughter from the car seat. She looked around and then buried her head back in her mother's neck and seemed to go back to sleep. Without thinking, he raised his hand to rub her back gently. A smile from Autumn was all the approval he needed, and his chest swelled with it.

"Perhaps you should start at the beginning, and we can take it from there?" Jack stood and walked to the door, putting his head out. "Lopez, Waggs, Deck, get your asses in here."

Relief washed through him knowing he'd have support from his brothers. Being an only child, he'd missed having siblings, and if he were honest, it had been the one thing he'd been unable to replace from his gang days until Eidolon. Then he'd seen the difference between his brothers from then and the ones he had now. His friends from long ago had been there as long as it suited them, but as soon as he turned his back on the gangs, he'd lost them too. He knew it had been for the best, but he'd missed that camaraderie until he'd met these men.

Waggs pushed through first, his eyes moving to Autumn then dropping to Maggie, the tensing of his muscles the only sign of surprise. Waggs was their medic and a former Army Green Beret. His story was a heart breaking one, and Mitch only knew it because he'd come home early one night and heard the music playing in his flat.

Worried, he'd knocked on the door and discovered a Waggs nobody else knew—at least nobody he knew of. Jack and Will probably knew the details of his tragic past, but he wasn't sure the rest of the team did, and Mitch would never betray him.

Lopez and Decker weren't far behind, Lopez with an easy smile and Decker instantly analysing the second he walked in the room. It was who he was, and although it was annoying as fuck half the time, the other half had saved them from some massive fuck ups. The man was like a human lie detector, clever to the point of brilliance. His brain didn't work like everyone else's did, rather it allowed him to see things that nobody else could.

"What's up?"

Waggs took a seat at the end of the conference table as Lopez sat in his usual chair beside the computer. Decker stayed in the corner of the room near the door, always on the peripheral.

"Autumn's in trouble, and we're gonna help her out." Jack's words were simple, but the meaning behind them was everything.

If Jack was willing to take this on, it meant two things—he'd see it through to the bitter end and the men after Autumn were more dangerous than he'd realised.

Chapter Nine

It was surreal to be surrounded by all of these powerful, deadly men. Mitch had hinted at how dangerous they were, but it was hard to understand it properly until you were in a room with them all. What was even more strange was that despite her baby girl being in her arms and her being so incredibly vulnerable, she didn't feel threatened or frightened by them.

Her breathing was calm, her heart beat with a steady, calm thud in her chest, not a single sense of fear invaded her body. She glanced at Mitch sitting beside her, noting the way he angled his body towards them in a protective gesture she wasn't sure he even realised he was making.

The rich, deep tone of his skin, a shade that was so beautifully intense, amplified the sable eyes that held her captive. Always so warm when they were on her, like a caress that heated her body, making her want to stretch like a cat lying in the warm sun of a lazy afternoon.

Feeling her eyes on him, he glanced her way, and those same eyes held so much reassurance. He would keep her safe, she'd bet her life on it and was, but she felt no hesitation. Autumn wondered if perhaps she trusted Mitch more than anyone she ever had. It was a strange thing to give someone you barely knew so much power, yet in her heart, Autumn knew it was right.

He tightened his grip on her fingers, giving the barest nod of reassurance before he turned back to the others in the room. She'd briefly met Waggs at the house. The man with short blond hair and cool, almost haunted eyes watched them as he leaned back in his chair—waiting. He seemed nice, held back a bit with her but with his friends he was one of them, a man who would protect.

Lopez was clearly the joker from what she could see, handsome and playful but with deep emotions. Then there was Decker. She didn't know what he did, but out of all of them, he gave her the most pause. She felt as if he were in her head, judging, waiting, analysing. He was also the only man wearing a suit, and even if it was without a tie, it still screamed control. The others wore a mix of jeans or combat trousers with t-shirts.

"I need you to tell us everything from the top, Autumn, including your real name."

She startled as Jack addressed her before lifting her chin and giving the barest of nods. The feel of Maggie in her arms and Mitch's steady hand in her own, giving her confidence. "I was born Keisha Anderson. I met my husband, Terrell Campbell in college. We were both studying chemistry. We got together and ended up going to Uni together. We were both studying the same degree, and we pushed each other to work harder. We were so competitive with each other." Autumn glanced at Mitch, watching for his reaction, feeling as if the walls were closing in on her as she talked about her past.

"Need some water?" Mitch asked with a dip of his head.

Autumn nodded. "Please."

Mitch went to move, but Waggs was already on his feet. "I'll get it."

Waggs was out the door before Mitch could reply. Moments later he was back and handing her a bottle of icy cold water. She hadn't known that reliving this would be so hard. She'd thought she'd processed all of her residual feelings of love and anger for Terrell until there was only apathy left.

Autumn took a sip and let the cold liquid calm her, the sense of being trapped started to recede, and her heartbeat began to calm. "Sorry, this is harder than I thought."

"Take your time. We aren't going anywhere and nobody in this room is judging you," Jack said from the end of the table where he was sitting with his arms relaxed on his lap.

Maggie wriggled and Autumn knew she didn't have long before her daughter woke properly and demanded feeding, so she hurried on. "We got married after college and both landed jobs at Orion Pharmaceuticals as Senior Research Scientists. It was the dream, and life was good, then his sister married a man called Anton Williams. I knew when I met him he was trouble, but I never imagined how much. Terrell got on well with him though, and they started spending more time together."

Autumn rubbed Maggie's back gently, not entirely sure who she was soothing with the motion. "Anton smoked a lot of weed, but as far as I knew nothing else, so I let it go. Then Terrell started missing work or coming home late, and I confronted him. I thought he was

53

cheating on me, but he said he wasn't and begged for a second chance."

Shrugging with embarrassment she continued, "I gave it to him, and we started trying for Maggie." She brushed her cheek over her daughter's curly hair. "Then I began to find discrepancies at work, chemicals missing, and drugs used to analyse the reaction to overdoses missing during Terrell's time in the lab. I went home to confront him, and we had a blazing fight about it. I begged him to stop, to come clean, and we'd face it together, but he said it was too late. He liked the power and the money, was sick of struggling to pay back student loans and scraping for every penny."

Autumn sighed, and her eyes caught on Mitch, drawing strength from him. "I decided that night I'd pack my bags and leave the next day. Terrell didn't like that, and he hit me, backhanding me across the face."

Autumn caught the lip twitch from Mitch, the squeeze of his fingers as he tried to control his reaction. "I knew then the man I had loved was gone. I stayed home the next day while he went to work. I was packing my stuff when he came home frantic, said the boss had found out he'd been skimming the drugs. He was terrified, but I had little sympathy, and then there was a hammering on the door like it was being caved in by some wild hoard. Terrell pushed me into the wardrobe and told me to keep silent."

Autumn grabbed the water and took another sip. "A man came into our bedroom and shot Terrell three times. He said this was what snitches got and nobody blabbed about the Onyx Cobras and then left." Autumn felt Mitch stiffen beside her, his hand withdrawing from hers as he crossed his arms.

"How did you end up in witness protection?" Waggs asked.

Autumn's eyes moved to him, and he was leaning forward, elbows on the table, his eyes intense.

Maggie began to wriggle, and without hesitation, Mitch put his arms out for her, and Autumn let him take her, offering him a grateful smile as she did, which he returned.

"The CPS begged me to testify, saying they'd protect me. Evidently, they'd been trying to get this guy for years."

"What went wrong?" Decker asked from across the room, where he stood, leaning against the wall as if he had little care for her answer.

"Someone took the gun used to kill Terrell out of evidence without authorisation, and the case fell apart. Linton Allen walked free, and I now have to live in fear of retribution from him and his men."

"Linton Allen?" Mitch bit out, shock on his face.

"Yes, he's the leader of the Cobras."

"Fuck." Mitch scrapped his hand over his short hair as he leaned over to give Maggie back to her. "I need some air."

Autumn watched as he paced to the door in long, quick strides as if the hounds of hell were after him.

Silence stole the oxygen from the room, and Autumn sat up straighter, suddenly feeling vulnerable and confused. She didn't know what had just happened with Mitch, but the name seemed to set him off. Was it possible he knew Linton Allen or had some dealings with him in the past? She didn't have a clue, and in that moment, she realised how very little she knew of the man who'd come to mean so much to her in the last few weeks.

As Maggie began to fuss and build up to a full-fledged tantrum, Autumn looked around the room at the men who were quietly talking. All of a sudden her life was out of control again. The desire to flee was almost cloying against her skin.

The door opened, and Autumn straightened hoping Mitch was back but instead saw the pretty detective who was her handler.

"Autumn." Aubrey's face lit up with a smile that had Autumn instantly relaxing. She walked towards her and crouched beside her chair, worried eyes on her face. "I had no idea you were Mitch's tenant."

Aubrey reached out a hand and stroked Maggie's cheek. It had been Aubrey who had watched Maggie while Autumn went and looked at the apartment in Mitch's house just over a month ago.

Autumn gave Aubrey a smile she didn't feel. "I guess this place is smaller than I thought."

Aubrey rolled her eyes. "You have no idea." Aubrey pulled her top lip between her teeth. "Jack says you're in trouble?"

"Anton Williams called me. He somehow got my number."

"Do you have the phone? We can see if there's anything on it to give us a clue to how he found you."

"Mitch has it."

Aubrey looked around the room. "And where is Mitch?"

Autumn shook her head. "He went to get some air."

Aubrey lifted her chin and then cast a glance at Jack. "Is there someplace Autumn can feed Maggie without an audience?"

Autumn felt the heat hit her cheeks as half the men in the room began to talk at the same time as they headed to the door, Decker and Lopez moving so fast it was a wonder they didn't leave skid marks.

Jack rolled his eyes as Alex calmly stood. "Follow me, Autumn, you can use my office."

Autumn looked at the handsome man with golden hair and nodded. Aubrey was by her side as Alex showed them to the space he called an office which contained a small couch behind a glass desk.

"Thank you."

Alex just nodded and backed out of the room without a word, leaving just her and Aubrey in the room.

"You should've called me," Aubrey chastised gently as Autumn fed her daughter.

"I know, but it all happened so quickly, and Mitch said they'd help and had more resources than the police." Autumn let her shoulders sag. "I'm just trying to do what's best for Maggie."

Aubrey rubbed her arm, offering comfort, as if sensing this had been an emotional day for her. "Mitch is right, they do have more resources and if they say they'll help, let them. My brother-in-law to be is a good man, and so are the others. They'll keep you safe. They saved my ass and Madison's." Aubrey looked around as if searching for something. "Speaking of Madison, did you notice my sister when you came in?"

Autumn shook her head. "No, sorry."

Aubrey threw her hands up. "It's fine. My sister is somewhat of a loose cannon."

"Yeah, I guess we all have a sibling like that."

"You too?"

Autumn nodded as she switched her daughter to the other boob. "Yeah, my younger brother. He's ten years younger than me and always seems to fall in with the wrong people. He has a good heart, but he's a sheep sometimes."

"That's Madison. Soooo, are you and Mitch a thing?" Aubrey asked with a secret smile.

Autumn blushed. The truth was she didn't really know what they were. There was a huge attraction between them, and they'd kissed several times but did that mean they were together?

Until now she'd have said a tentative yes, but with him walking out the way he had, she wasn't so sure. Autumn glanced at Aubrey. She barely knew the woman but sensed she could be a good friend.

She shrugged. "I'm not sure what we are. I'd thought we had something, but then he bailed halfway through the meeting like his ass was on fire."

Aubrey tipped her head as she looked at Autumn. "Can I give you a little advice, woman to woman?"

"Sure, not like I have anyone else to give it."

Aubrey reached out and laid a hand on her arm before withdrawing it when she had Autumn's full attention. "These men," she waved a hand in the air behind her, "are fierce protectors. They work hard, play hard, and are the most loyal you'll ever find. When they make any kind of commitment to be there, to protect you or to love you, they take it seriously. What they aren't is great at accepting they can't control everything." Aubrey gave a low chuckle. "Believe me, Will is the best man I know, and I love him with every bone in my body, but sometimes I want to strangle him because he thinks he can fix everything and we know as women we don't necessarily need them to fix it, but to be there."

Autumn fixed her top as she sat Maggie on her lap, the baby offering Aubrey a beautiful smile. Aubrey reached over and took her hand, seemingly thoroughly enthralled as everyone was who met Maggie.

"Are you saying Mitch walked out because he wants to fix it and can't?"

"Maybe or maybe it isn't only about you. All of these men have baggage. They're warriors, after all. Just talk to him, find out what's going on in his head before you kick his ass."

Autumn laughed then and was still laughing when Mitch walked in moments later and she was glad for it, he needed to see her strength for a change.

Chapter Ten

The name had been like a punch to the guts, it had never crossed his mind that Linton Allen could be the man who was hunting Autumn and Maggie. The thought made him physically sick to the point he'd had to get out of there before he threw up or passed out like a fucking pussy.

As he'd sat out the back wishing like fuck he still smoked, his mind had fallen back over twenty-five years to the last time he'd seen Linton Allen standing over the grave of Mitch's best friend and Linton's older brother Devon. They'd both been wearing black.

His friend's death had wrecked Mitch, but in part out of guilt. Devon had been pulled deeper and deeper into the Cobras, and Mitch kept pulling away until a gulf separated them. He'd felt so powerless, so angry at everyone for his inner conflict but Linton had been so much younger then. Barely ten years old, a good kid who stayed out of trouble—Devon had known enough about what he was getting involved with to try and keep his younger brother away.

That was the pain that plagued Mitch to this day. He now knew he'd wanted out but had found himself in too deep, and instead of helping him, Mitch had saved his own ass and turned his back. He hadn't realised it then of course, but now it was as clear as crystal Devon had needed his help, he'd needed his best friend but hadn't known how to ask—shouldn't have had to ask for it.

He blew out a breath and twisted his head as Waggs walked towards him, hands in his pockets, his head tipped to the sun before his eyes met his.

Mitch held up a hand to stop whatever was coming. "Don't say it."

Waggs sat beside him on the long bench that faced the training field and the assault course. To the left was the beginning of the new dog squad quarters. When Jack made a decision, he didn't fuck around.

Waggs stayed silent, as was his way, always letting people talk if they needed it. He wasn't much on words himself, which was probably why they got along so well.

"Is she okay?" Mitch couldn't help but ask.

He had to explain but how could he tell her that he could've stopped this from happening if only he'd been a better friend?

"She's stronger than she looks."

Mitch nodded before rubbing his hand over his short hair. "Yeah, I know, but I just finished telling her how she could trust me, and then I behave like that."

Waggs winced a little. "Not great timing but I'm sure she'll get over it."

"Yeah well, she shouldn't have to." Mitch was angry with himself for letting her down so quickly after promising not to.

"You're too hard on yourself, Mitch. You're human. We fuck shit up. If she's worth it, she'll understand that this won't be the last time and she'll make mistakes too. It's life."

Mitch looked out at the helipad on the opposite side of the complex, his mind mulling over Waggs' words. "What about you, Waggs? You always hold yourself to such a high standard. You don't allow yourself to make mistakes." The pain that flashed across Waggs face almost took his breath away, and Mitch was sorry for his words, regret hitting him fast. "I'm sorry, I shouldn't have said that."

Waggs waved his hand as he looked at the ground. "Forget it, but the truth is, I can't afford mistakes. If I fuck up someone dies, and I can't have that on my conscience. The weight of any more deaths at my door is just too heavy."

"Do you ever think about settling down?" Mitch asked, surprised by Waggs opening up that much.

Waggs stood and blocked the sun with his back, making him look aloof and dangerous. "Nah, not for me. Too much risk involved. Easier to jump out of a plane or chase down a terrorist than find a woman who's willing to take on my shit." Waggs scratched his stubble. "You, though, I can see you and a woman like Autumn making it work. She has spirit, and you need that."

Mitch smiled. "Yeah, I do."

Mitch stood as Waggs walked towards the new K9 unit. He needed to explain his behaviour to Autumn and then figure out a way to keep her and Maggie safe, even if it meant killing his oldest friend's brother.

He found her in Alex's office laughing with Aubrey, and his muscles relaxed a fraction at the uninhibited sound of her laughter.

Her eyes met his as he walked in, the connection they shared as strong as ever.

"Can we talk?" he asked, aiming his eyes at Autumn—she'd always be Autumn to him. Keisha didn't fit the woman he knew at all, nor did the career she'd chosen, but that was irrelevant.

"Yes, sure."

"Want me to take Maggie for a few minutes? We can go annoy Lopez and Jack."

Autumn grinned, her entire face lighting up like a rainbow after a storm. "That would be great."

"No problem."

Aubrey smiled, taking Maggie and hitching her to her hip like a natural. He wondered how long it would before she and Will made it official and began a family.

With his hands in his pockets, he moved closer to Autumn as the silence in the room took over, feeling awkward for the first time since they'd met, that it was his own doing made it an even harder pill to swallow. "I'm sorry."

Autumn looked up in surprise at his words, but the wariness he saw there slayed him.

"You don't owe me an explanation, Mitch."

He crossed to her, hating the space between them, and sat close beside her, taking her hand. The callouses on her hand from gardening only making her more beautiful to him. Her warm bronze skin was clear and perfect as he brushed her cheek with his other hand.

"I do, Autumn, don't say that. I want us to be an us, and that includes me not acting like a dick at the first sign of trouble."

Her brows furrowed, but she left her hand in his, leaned her cheek into his touch. "What trouble? Have I caused you problems with my own?"

Mitch shook his head. "No, not at all. The opposite in fact."

"Mitch, I don't understand. Just spit it out."

He grinned at her no-nonsense words, reminding him of the women in his family. "Fuck me, you're perfect."

"Whatever."

He stifled the grin that wanted to break free and wondered at her ability to change his mood from dark to light with just a simple sentence. "I know Linton Allen."

Her eyes went wide, and he could feel the tension cascade down her shoulders to her hands, so he moved closer.

"I was best friends with his brother growing up. We went to the same school, lived a few doors away from each other, and our mothers were friends. When Devon was eleven his mum died, and his dad moved in, allegedly to take care of him, but I think it was so he could claim the council flat. Devon started hanging out later and later at night with the older kids."

He gave a dry laugh. "My Ma was strict, which I hated at the time, but she saved my life. Devon got involved with the Onyx Cobras, and we drifted apart. Then when he was around fifteen, he began to reach out to me more. We mainly played computer games and talked about girls, but it felt good to have him back. Then he got shot by a rival gang and died. His younger brother Linton was a good kid. Great grades, smart as hell, and Devon kept him away from the gangs."

Autumn was leaning into him, her hand on his forearm, gripping it tightly. "What happened?"

Mitch sighed. "After the funeral, my mum got us out of there. She didn't want me anywhere near the gang, so she took a job forty miles away on some big estate as a housekeeper. I finished up at a local school, and she cut all my ties with my old friends."

"That must have been hard."

"It was, but she saved my life. I have zero doubt I'd have ended up dead had I stayed. Instead, Mum met a great guy, and I joined the force."

"I'm guessing there's more to this story than that."

Her chuckle made his dick hard, the warm sound wrapping around him like a silk glove. "There is, but my point is, I saved myself and left Linton to fend for himself. If I'd stayed or taken more notice of what it meant when Devon reached out, I might've seen he needed me and been able to help."

"Mitch, don't be silly. Of course you couldn't, you were a child. No kid should take on a weight like that. Devon is a tragedy in our society, and so is Linton to a degree, but both could've made different choices and didn't."

"Do you believe that? That it's a choice for some kids?"

"Every single thing we do is a choice, what to wear, what to eat. Linton chose to join the gang that got his brother killed." Autumn shrugged throwing up her hands. "Maybe to avenge his brother, I don't know, but killing people to avenge a life is on him."

"Autumn, I've killed people. This job is not without its sacrifices." He needed her to know the man he was before they went any further.

"And I trust you make them for the greater good, not for money or greed. That is my choice, right or wrong. Although I have a feeling it's closer to the wild imaginings I had about a secret black ops group than I thought."

"We work for the British Government and the Palace, and that's as much as I can say. The rest is classified."

"See super-secret spy shit. So, I guess you guys really are best placed to help me figure this out if Jack is willing."

"If he weren't, you wouldn't still be here."

Autumn's eyes bulged. "He'd kill me?"

Mitch threw back his head and laughed. "Of course not, I meant he'd have made you leave."

"Oh, thank god."

He bent his head closer, his lips touching hers as her breath hitched. "I'm so glad you chose to rent my apartment."

"Me too."

He kissed her hard and deep, their tongues tangling, breath melding as desire poured through his veins, the little sounds of pleasure she made in her throat driving him crazy with need.

He pulled back to look at her glassy eyes heavy with desire. "I want you."

"I want you too. Will you stay with me tonight?"

"Was going to anyway, babe, but if you mean in your bed then fuck yes. That's an invitation I'm happy to accept."

Chapter Eleven

"So, what happens now?" Autumn was happy despite the situation she found herself in now. Having things cleared up with Mitch meant more to her than she realised. The man had gotten under her skin in the last few weeks. He'd become vital to her mental wellbeing in a way she hadn't known until things had seemed shaky between them.

Walking back towards the conference room where she'd met some of the guys earlier, Mitch had Maggie back, having retrieved her from Aubrey when she'd had to leave on an urgent call.

"Now we find out where Linton is and exactly what's going on with the Onyx Cobras."

"I still can't believe you know him." Autumn was still processing that news and everything he'd told her about his past.

Mitch frowned. "That's just it. I don't know him, not now. Linton was a good kid, extremely bright, and that's a bad thing for us."

Taking the seat she'd had before she was slightly surprised that they were letting her in on this meeting but grateful too. She'd spent the last two years almost feeling as if she had no control over what happened to her and Maggie. These men were giving her that by allowing her to be part of her own future.

Waggs and Lopez moved in next, followed by Alex, Jack, and another man she didn't know who had tattoos on every visible surface of his skin. He, like Lopez, was carrying a laptop.

"Will, this is Autumn and Maggie." Mitch swung his arm between her and the previously unknown man. "Autumn, this is Will, geek extraordinaire."

Will grinned at her. "Good to meet you, Autumn." He settled near the bank of computers and hooked up his laptop.

"Nice to meet you too. You're Aubrey's husband?"

He shook his head. "Not yet, but as soon as I can pin her down on a date, I will be."

"Speaking of which," Alex began causing the team to turn to him, "Evelyn and I set a date for the New Year."

His smile was full, and without even knowing him well or meeting Evelyn, Autumn was happy for them. Congratulations echoed around the room from the others, and she felt the genuine affection between these robust operators.

"Now we know we have a party to look forward to at the end of the year, let's make sure all our shit is dealt with before then." Jack pursed his lips as he eyed Will. "Will, do you want to tell us what you know about Linton Allen and the Onyx Cobras?"

Will's fingers moved over the keyboard like lightning as he directed their gazes to the screen behind them. Autumn turned and caught Mitch dodging a wet fist from her daughter, a relaxed smile on his face before it fell at the sight of Linton on the screen.

She fought the shiver of fear snaking down her spine at the sight of the man who'd so carelessly and calmly murdered her husband as he walked across the road on the image. He was tall, good looking some would say, with dark mahogany skin and hazel green eyes. Linton Allen was lean and muscled, and his stride, even frozen in time on the image, screamed arrogance.

"That's not the kid I knew," Mitch said with a sorrowful tone.

"Yeah, that's the truth. Linton Allen joined the Cobras at fifteen. He rose quickly through the ranks and rumour is he's brutal and swift with his punishment, often carrying out his own hits." Will gave a quick look of apology to Autumn but carried on. "He trusts very few people, only those closest to him, which is Midas, their accountant and Hench, his second." Two more images appeared on the screen, neither of which she knew.

"As far as I can tell, Anton Williams is mid-level but a bit of a climber. He wants to be top-level but has neither the intelligence nor the stomach for what the Cobras are into now."

Mitch glanced at her as Maggie wriggled, Autumn leaned in and took her daughter as if it were the most natural thing in the world for her to do. He offered her a wink which had her clenching her legs with desire even as the heat warmed her face.

"Which is?"

Mitch leaned back in his seat as Waggs asked the question.

"Drugs and guns. Intel says that the Cobras have been coming up in connection to arms deals made with Pakistan, Iran, and Saudi Arabia."

Mitch swung his head to Jack. "Where the fuck are they getting enough weapons to satisfy that sort of demand?"

"This is where it gets interesting and complicated. Allen, as you know, was brilliant and joining the Cobras didn't change that. We can't find any links to a pipeline coming into the country, but we can find a tenuous link to a known exporter." Jack rested his elbows on the table, fingers clasped.

"So how is he getting the guns?" Waggs' jaw clenched as he spoke, and Autumn could feel the anger coming from him.

"Here's where it gets fuzzy. I found a transaction linking Anton to the purchase of this property here." He flicked his head at the screen, which showed a large cluster of warehouses in the middle of a farm. "This is a farm owned by Henderson Corp."

The image changed again, and Autumn's heart jumped into her throat when she saw her dead husband walking into the building beside Allen and Anton. Her chest tightened, nausea climbing up her throat as the betrayal in front of her manifested in her chest. A hand on her arm grounded her, the warmth of Mitch's touch holding her together as her nerves frayed at the edges.

"How are Henderson Corp and Anton linked?" Mitch demanded.

"Henderson bought it but transferred it to Anton's name straight after purchase."

"That makes no sense." Waggs crossed his arms and blew out a breath and angled his head to Lopez. "What do we know about Henderson Corp?"

"They make pesticides for agricultural farming. The owner, Verena Finch, is the daughter of Harold Charles who owns Orion Pharmaceuticals."

Autumn drew in a sharp breath at the link to her old company. There was something she was missing, but she couldn't figure out what or why.

"Henderson was formed when Finch married her second husband four years ago. Rumour is her father didn't approve, and they had a huge falling out. Her husband Trenton has a background in farming and agriculture, and they set up the company shortly after they were married."

"I still don't understand what this has to do with Allen and Anton." Autumn looked at Mitch and then Lopez. "How does farming link to weapons and drugs?"

65

"I'm not sure yet."

Mitch ran his thumb over his full lips in concentration, and the movement made her lose her own. Even seated with tension rolling off his broad shoulders, she could see the sensuality in the man. He was an arresting sight and one which she'd never get tired of looking at she feared. Yet, what was coming to light in this meeting was that a can of worms was open and spilling everywhere at her feet. This mess was so much bigger than she'd realised, believing that it was a simple murder trial when it had to be more than that.

"We held chemicals at the lab that are used in pesticides that have to be controlled and documented for every use. One of the discrepancies I found with Terrell involved one called CH5N. Its main use is for crops, but its formula is very similar to that of Tabun."

Autumn let her sentence hang not sure what she was trying to say but hoping one of these men would pick up the thread of her thoughts.

Will glanced at her, his eyes alive before they dropped back to the monitor as he began to type like a man possessed. "She's right, and if that is the case, what are the chances that the Cobras aren't moving physical weapons but chemical ones?"

A hushed silence fell over the room, the only sound Maggie cooing on her knee as the magnitude of the implication penetrated.

"We need eyes on that warehouse, and I need a full report on anything to do with Henderson, Finch, Orion, Allen, and the Cobras now!" Jack jabbed the table with his forefinger, his face a controlled mask, but his eyes a stormy grey.

"What about Autumn?" Mitch draped his arm over the back of her chair in a protective gesture which made her anxiety ease a little.

"Autumn, is it possible Terrell was involved in making chemical weapons?" Jack clasped his fingers together as he looked at her.

Autumn raised both eyebrows, her hands smoothing the creases from her little girl's purple dress as she thought about the question. "It's possible. Terrell was a brilliant chemist, but I find it hard to believe he'd be involved with that."

"Yet he was involved in drugs, and you found that acceptable?" Decker asked with a crisp edge to his tone as he stepped forward.

"Decker, that's enough." Mitch glared at the man, his voice a growl of warning.

Decker shrugged his shoulders and tipped his head. "It was an observation."

"Yeah well, fucking keep them to yourself."

Autumn laid a hand on Mitch's leg, and he glanced at her. "It's okay, he's protecting you. I get that." She looked at Decker. "In answer to your observation, I didn't find it acceptable at all. Anyone that deals in drugs is abhorrent, but it's a hard pill to swallow to imagine that the man you loved, the father of your child, was involved in making and producing chemical weapons. I grew up surrounded by drug dealers, so it's an easier step for me to take, whereas this isn't. So, to answer your question with an open mind rather than an emotional one, then yes, Terrell could've been involved."

Decker gave a small nod, a smile twitching his lips. Autumn had a distinct impression that few people challenged him or his cunning insight.

"Wow, she totally schooled you, Deck." Lopez laughed, which gained him a glare from Decker.

"Can we get back to the problem at hand and the reason we're meeting." Mitch threw up his hands but offered her a small grin of respect.

"Yes, let's do that. I have somewhere to be tonight." Jack gave Mitch and Alex a glance but said no more.

"Mitch, it goes without saying you're on protection detail, but I want Waggs with you on that. I know security at your place is tight but I'd recommend you keep all outdoor activity to a minimum until we can have eyes on all the players and get them under surveillance.

"Alex, I need you to get us operational control on this. Find out whose radar the Cobras are on and speak to the Palace if necessary so we can control the external factors. I don't want to fuck up any long term investigation or op, but this is a matter of National Security and falls under our remit."

Alex stood. "On it." Alex grinned at Autumn before swiping a gentle hand over Maggie's head. "Good to meet you, ladies."

"You too, Alex."

"Will, can you help Lopez and also figure out how Anton found Autumn?"

Will grinned at his brother. "I can. Are you asking if I will?"

Jack shook his head and blew out a long-suffering breath. "Don't bust my balls on this."

"But it's so much fun." Will chuckled as he walked to the door, making Autumn laugh at the banter between the brothers.

"Deck, you know what to do. Oh, and before I forget, Madison handed in her notice already." Jack glared at Mitch. "Apparently she's going to nursing school."

Mitch smirked. "What? She said she wanted to be a nurse, and we all knew she hated this job. I saved you from wasting your time training her up."

"Yeah except now I have no admin support, and I'm back looking for staff as well as the other hundred things I need to do."

"I can do it," Autumn said before her brain had even engaged.

Jack and Mitch both looked at her, pinning her with an eagle eye. "I'm used to admin tasks, did my certification in editing and business while I was pregnant and in hiding. Plus, you already know my background."

"You're hired." Jack slapped the table and stood, the first real smile on his face and boy, the man was fine.

Mitch laid a hand on her arm, concern in his warm brown eyes. "Are you sure about this? It's a lot to take on, and you have Maggie."

"I can bring her with me, can't I?" She glanced at Jack for confirmation.

"Sure, as long as the work gets done here, I don't care if you work around your daughter and bring her with you."

She glanced back to Mitch. "See, it's fine and this way you don't have to worry about me not being safe when you're at work. You and Waggs can carry on as normal in the day and Maggie and I are safe at Fort Knox."

"If that's what you want." Mitch still looked perturbed, but she didn't call him on it.

"You'll need to sign an NDA before you start, but Lopez can sort that out."

Jack strode from the room but stopped at the door addressing Mitch. "Can you arrange cover for tonight or do you want me to take someone else?"

Again, Autumn got the feeling this was over her head.

"I can ask Nate or Bebe if they're free."

68

"Fine." Then Jack was gone.

"Want to get that ice cream now?" Mitch asked with a grin, and Autumn returned it.

This man was dangerous in so many ways but only to her heart.

Chapter Twelve

Mitch rested his elbow on the car window as he watched the deserted area around the abandoned farm. The sky was dark, with only a crescent moon to offer any light. Luckily, he had his NVGs if he needed them, but this should be a quick meet. A tendril of unease crept down his spine as they waited, the meeting time coming and going.

"He's late," he said stating the obvious, knowing Jack and Alex would pick it up on the comms, even as he spoke to Waggs and Decker who were in the car with him.

Waggs was sitting in the front beside him. "It's only a few minutes."

Mitch turned to Waggs his brow raised. "Have you ever known Gunner to be late?"

"Did we ever know Gunner at all?" Waggs asked with a sardonic lift of his brow.

Mitch wasn't sure how to respond to that, so he didn't. The fact was, Gunner had betrayed them all, throwing everything back in their faces. Fuck, he'd even knocked him out and tied him up when he'd confronted him about the op in Monaco. It was a bitter pill to swallow to know someone he'd trusted with his life had been the one sabotaging everything.

Yet Mitch understood on some level. The bastards had threatened his sister, kidnapped her from the nursing home where she was cared for after a brain injury had left her unable to care for herself.

Would he have done the same? He hoped not. He hoped he would've been a better man. These men were as much family as his blood were. Gunner choosing to go against them rather than trusting them to have his back had almost ripped the team to shreds. Only Jack being the leader he was had kept the team together.

"You think we can trust him?" Mitch asked the million-dollar question.

"No," Waggs answered sharply.

Mitch lifted his head to the rearview mirror to look at Decker. "What about you? You're the shrink, what do you think?"

Decker's lips tightened. Mitch knew he hated when they called him that. "I think there's something else going on we don't know about."

"Like what?" Mitch asked, surprised by this analysis.

"I don't know, but something. The Gunner I knew would've come to us about his sister."

"Even though he kept her a secret?" Waggs asked.

"Yes. Because from everything I've seen, Gunner still trusts us, despite how it looks."

"Yeah well, that shit doesn't go both ways," Waggs snarled as he checked the time on his watch.

As he did headlights slashed through the night sky and the tension in the car rose, electricity pounding out of them.

"Heads up, boys," Jack said over the comms as Gunner stopped the old car close to the old, metal silage barn. He got out and instantly Mitch could see something was wrong. Gunner staggered before falling to his knees.

"Waggs, get out here now," Jack demanded through their ears as he stepped forward to grab Gunner.

All three men were out of the car and running towards Jack and Gunner as Alex covered Jack's back. Mitch had his gun in his hand, not trusting this wasn't a trap of some kind. When they got to the two men, Gunner was on the ground. His face was barely recognisable and covered in blood. He had a cut above his eyebrow and a broken nose by the looks of it but Mitch suspected it was the injuries he couldn't see that were causing the most problems.

Waggs was on his knees, his medic training kicking in as he triaged Gunner, lifting his shirt to show his abdomen covered in so many bruises it looked like one giant injury. "What the fuck happened to you?"

Gunner tried to brush his hand away. "It's fine."

Waggs ignored him. "Don't be a dick. Let me check you over. You could have internal injuries."

"Nah, just some broken ribs."

Jack was standing slightly back, assessing things with Alex. "Let him check you over, Gunner." The words were harsh and commanding and seemed to get through to Gunner because he fell back to the ground with a grunt.

Mitch kept his eye on the surrounding area, knowing Jack was doing the same as Alex walked around the back of the car. Lopez had them on camera from the drones he was using remotely.

Trust was a hard-won commodity in this job and even more so now.

He thought of Autumn and Maggie, hoping they were tucked up safely in bed. Nate had offered to stay with her once Mitch—with her permission—had shared her situation with him. With Liam, Reid, and Blake being on a recon op in Belize after a contact gave them a tip about increasing violence against the Crown, they were short on bodies. With the Royal tour next year, it was vital they stay on top of these things, and that included wrapping up this threat from inside.

Waggs looked up. "He needs an MRI scan."

"No." Gunner started to sit up, his breath hitching as he bit back grunts of pain.

"What happened?" Jack folded his arms over his chest, his face a stony mask of anger.

"I had to prove I was loyal to them. They tortured me until they were satisfied I wasn't working with you."

"Fuck sake," Mitch growled causing Gunner to look at him through one open eye. "Who did this?"

Gunner looked down, spitting out blood from his mouth. "Bás but he had no choice or he would've blown his cover." Gunner glanced at Waggs. "That's why I know no internal stuff is fucked up. He pulled his punches. Listen, I haven't got a lot of time, they'll be watching me closely now. I met the boss, and you won't fucking believe who it is."

The tension seemed to magnify. It was so thick that you could almost touch it in the air around them.

"Tell me," Jack ordered as all eyes went to Gunner.

"Osbourne."

"Deputy Commissioner Osbourne?" Waggs asked incredulity lacing his tone.

"Yeah, met him earlier. He wants you out so he can put his own men in our," he paused for a second, "your places."

"That bastard." Alex paced, showing a rare moment of fury.

"He must have someone inside the Palace, though."

"He has his men," Mitch offered as his own anger unfurled in his belly. He should be used to it by now—money was so often the source of conflict or war, yet he still found it hard to understand.

"No, higher up than that. We need to talk to Fitz and perhaps even consider Fitz as the source."

"I don't like him for this." Decker was walking around the car after Alex had run a wand over it looking for bugs or bombs and finding none.

"Who then?"

"Not sure but Fitz is loyal to the Queen and she's loyal to us."

"Everyone has a price," Waggs said as he straightened and held out a hand to help Gunner up. They fell silent as the meaning behind his words settled over them.

"I should go." Gunner stepped towards the driver's side.

Jack followed him. "You need to pull out, this is too dangerous. You could get killed next time."

Gunner shook his head. "No, it's fine. I need to find out who the insider in the Palace is and I think Osbourne has a partner. Bás agrees with me."

"You and Bás best friends now or what?"

Mitch frowned not liking this turn. He didn't trust the Irishman's sudden appearance in all of this. The man was a true ghost, not even Will could find him, and that was a dangerous place for the team to be especially as he'd been the man to torture Siren—Alex's woman.

His link to Osiris, the largest Heroin dealer in the US and Europe and the man who'd hidden under the radar for so long before Roz and Zenobi had eliminated him for hurting one of their own, was reason enough to distrust him. Now Gunner seemed to be allying himself with him too. It made Mitch's skin crawl to think one of their own was in such a precarious position, but then he remembered Gunner wasn't Eidolon any longer.

"No, but we have the same goals."

"We had the same goals, that didn't stop you before." Mitch pointed to his chest with emphasis.

Gunner's jaw went hard, the verbal blow landing where Mitch had meant it too. "Do you think I don't fucking know that? I fucked up and now I'm trying to fix it."

"How?" Jack stepped closer his head tilted, the light showing the tension on his face. Gunner held his gaze, not flinching but Decker must have seen something they didn't

Decker moved in for the kill, his voice low and calm. "You're hiding something."

Mitch saw the sweat bead on Gunner's brow from the lights on the car. Decker was right; he was hiding something.

Jack grabbed him by his shirt and shoved him against the car, causing Gunner to wince from the injuries he'd sustained. "Lie to me one more time, mother fucker," Jack nodded to his face, "and this will be the least of your problems."

Mitch couldn't remember the last time he'd seen Jack lose his cool.

Gunner's face reddened, but he didn't attempt to fight back. "I can't tell you. Just tell Will to look into Miqdaad al-Sabir."

Jack dropped him like he was on fire. His boss looked shocked, distraught even. "How do you know that name?"

"How do you think?"

Jack paced away, brushing his hand over his face. "He's dead. We killed him on our first Eidolon op."

Mitch remembered it all too well; it had been his first visit to Parwan Province in Afghanistan, also known as the *Sandbox* and Bagram Airbase.

They'd landed late at night and joined a Seal Team to take down the high ranking Taliban leader Miqdaad al-Sabir. The op had been a success with the Seal Team providing support as it was an unsanctioned mission. Nobody ever knew Eidolon were involved. It had been clean and quick, with only their target and his men killed in the raid.

Jack whirled to face Gunner, who was observing him. "He's dead."

"Yes, but his son Samir isn't, and he took over last year when he turned twenty and is more vicious than his father ever was."

Waggs crossed his arms, angling his eyes at Gunner. "What has any of this got to do with the Palace or Osbourne?"

"You think Osbourne is working with Samir?" Jack asked.

Gunner nodded slowly. "I have to provide security for Osbourne on a trip to Germany next month where he's meeting with him. Then

I can confirm and also find out who his partner is as he's the one facilitating it."

"I'll have Will look into Samir al-Sabir." Jack fixed his eyes on Gunner. "But if you hold anything more back from me, then this arrangement is over, and you can kiss seeing your sister again goodbye." Jack left the threat hanging in the warm night air.

Gunner straightened, his jaw hardening. "Don't pull that on me, Jack. We both know harming innocents isn't how you operate."

"Maybe I'll make an exception this time."

Mitch knew he wouldn't, that wasn't Jack and certainly not him, but Gunner was a loose cannon and he was getting himself in deeper than he should be, and it could cost him his life.

"If they figure out you're playing them, they'll kill you." Mitch knew people like that; the chances were they'd kill him anyway once they were finished with him.

Gunner glanced at him with a shrug. "So be it." Then he turned to Jack. "You know why I kept this quiet until I was sure." With those words, he got in the car with a muffled groan of pain, reminding them of the beating he'd taken to get this information. "I'll be in touch."

The tires crunched on the dry earth as the headlights swung around before disappearing into the night.

"I want a meeting at 0800 to debrief." Jack turned to Alex. "Arrange for Blake, Reid, and Liam to be included on a video link." Jack was already walking away as he gave the command.

Mitch didn't like the feeling in the pit of his gut; it had always served him well in the past to listen to it, and now it was screaming something was wrong. He just didn't know if it was to do with Gunner or Autumn.

Chapter Thirteen

"Knock, knock." Jack popped his head around the door of her new office before stepping inside.

"Hi." Autumn swivelled from the computer in front of her on the sleek glass desk and faced her new boss, who was now seated in the chair on the other side of her desk, his posture relaxed as he leaned back, legs spread in front of him.

"I just wanted to check you have everything you need."

Autumn looked around at the office Mitch had shown her to this morning and let out a nervous laugh, throwing up her hands. "Are you kidding?" She looked at the travel cot in the corner, the baby play station that was still boxed up against the wall, and the playmat before her gaze fell back on Jack. "I can't believe you did all this."

Jack shrugged his shoulders, brushing off the kindness. "With you bringing Maggie in, I wanted to make sure you have everything you need to make this work."

"I have more than enough. It's very kind of you."

"Not really. I just don't want to give you a reason to leave when you see the amount of work that needs doing." His warm chuckle filled the room.

"I just need to gain access to some of these files then I can run some reports and see where we are with things."

Jack nodded once. "Lopez will be in shortly to set up your computer and access to things. There will be some things that are strictly confidential for Alex or me, but as time progresses, we can discuss that. Are you good with the filing side of things? I'd like most things filed in our secure cloud with as minimal paper as possible."

"Yes, I understand confidentiality. My last job was the same. I can scan a lot of this and get it on the cloud but the rest I can file using the system Madison set up."

Jack stood. "I'll need your bank details to pay your salary."

"I'll email them over." Autumn felt good having a purpose, not that having Maggie wasn't the best reason in the world, but it didn't stimulate her brain, and she'd realised she needed more than that.

Jack walked to the door, glancing at a sleeping Maggie as he did, his lips twitching up. "Oh, to sleep the sleep of the innocent."

Autumn got up and walked towards him. "Can I ask you something?" She wasn't sure if he'd answer, but she was curious.

"You can ask, no saying I'll answer."

Autumn nodded, tipping her head. "Fair enough. Why are you doing all this? Helping me, giving me a job." She twisted her fingers around the length of her hair, guilt swarming her that she'd doubted his kind intentions.

Jack looked at her intently as if he weighed up his answer before he spoke. "Eidolon is more than a bunch of men who work for me. They're family, you can't put yourself in the kind of danger we do and not know you'd die to protect your teammate. When you have that level of commitment, you stop being teammates and become brothers. Mitch is my brother, and you mean a lot to him, so that means you mean a lot to us now too."

"Wow, I don't know what to say to that."

"Don't get me wrong, the fact we get to take down this dangerous group is also a big factor, but we'd already decided before we knew the details."

"And the job, is it a pity job?"

Jack laughed. "Only in that you're taking pity on me. As you can see, I'm up shit creek with my paperwork."

Autumn laughed as she looked at the boxes of filing around her. "Well, filing is a guilty pleasure."

"I guess it's a win-win for everyone."

The door behind him opened, causing Jack to turn towards the sound. A woman with beautiful red hair poked her head in and smiled. "Pax, what can we do for you?" Jack sounded amused.

"I thought perhaps Autumn might need a hand getting settled in the job."

The woman called Pax walked in, looking elegant and sophisticated, her blush pink dress moulded to her body. Autumn looked down at her own bohemian dress of petrol blue with orange flowers, simple V-neck and floaty short sleeves, and wondered if it was a bit too grunge.

Pax walked straight towards her, a broad grin on her beautiful face. "Wow, I love this dress, it's so pretty."

77

Autumn started as the woman pulled her in for a hug before she returned it somewhat awkwardly. "Thanks, I love yours too."

Autumn looked at Jack as another woman walked inside. She was shorter than Pax with long dark hair and full lips.

Jack cocked his head as he crossed his arms. "Evelyn, you too?"

"We just wanted to say hello."

Evelyn, she remembered, was Alex's fiancée.

"Callie, Taamira, you might as well come on in, I know you're out there," Jack called.

Two more women stepped through the door and into the now crowded office at Jack's command looking sheepish.

Jack turned to her. "On that note, I'll leave you to it."

In moments he was gone closing the door with an eye roll for Pax.

"That man needs to loosen up," Pax drawled her American accent cultured.

Autumn lifted her hand to rest on the pram where Maggie still slept as four pairs of eyes fell on her.

The other two women were equally beautiful, and it took her a second to figure it out, but one was Calista Lund.

"Hi, I'm Callie. It's nice to meet you."

She took the proffered hand and shook it silently, feeling somewhat lost for words and for once hoping Maggie would wake up and steal all the attention.

"She knows who you are, Callie. Look at her face."

Autumn blinked and looked at Evelyn. "Yeah, sorry."

"I'm Evelyn, this is Pax, Callie, who you know, and this is Princess Taamira, but you can call her Taamira."

"It's nice to meet you?" Autumn wasn't sure if her words were a question or a statement at this point.

Mitch was out of the office all day and wouldn't be back until early that evening as he and Decker had a meeting with someone in Gloucester. Jack had left her so she was on her own with these four women, and honestly, she hated situations like these.

She'd always got on with people at school but being the focus of attention and especially when that attention was from four gorgeous women, one of which was a model and the other a Princess, she wasn't comfortable.

78

Princess Taamira moved closer, and it was hard not to be affected by the knowledge she was royalty, especially encased in such beauty. She took Autumn's hands. "This is a lot, is it not? I know from when I met my Liam, it was scary to be bombarded by such confidence. Rest assured we mean well. We just wish you to know we are here and wish to be your friends."

"Why?" The single word was sharper than she intended, but her awkwardness was making her words come out wrong.

"Why?" Pax asked with a tilt of her head which caused her wavy hair to fall over her bare shoulder.

"Why do you want to be my friends?"

"Aubrey and Bebe said she was a spunky one." Evelyn laughed before she made herself at home in the chair Jack had vacated. Autumn's ear pricked at the names of two women she knew and liked already.

"You're with Mitch, right?" Callie asked.

"Well, yes, kind of. It's all very new." Autumn started moving the pram slightly as Maggie stirred.

"I'm with Reid, Pax is with Blake, Evelyn is engaged to Alex, and Taamira is with Liam. We're the Eidolon WAGs."

"WAGs?"

"Wives and girlfriends."

"Oh, I see."

"I hate when you use that term." Pax took a seat on the small couch that was along the left wall, and Taamira and Callie did the same as Autumn escaped behind her desk now that Maggie had gone back into a deep sleep.

"Well, what else would you call us?"

Pax twirled her hand. "Anything but that. It makes us sound like footballer's wives, or worse, Waggs' harem."

Callie giggled as her eyes went wide, her hand covering her mouth. "Oh my god, I hadn't even thought of that. Yeah, we definitely need a new name."

Autumn had never had an encounter like this, but she liked Bebe and Aubrey and if they all knew each other, then it had to mean something. "So, you all know each other well?"

"Pax and Evelyn work together, but they were super kind when I met Reid. Then we pounced on T when she met Liam. Our men are amazing, and I love Reid to death but having these three as friends has been one of the best things to come from everything that happened."

"What happened?" Autumn sat and leaned forward as her natural curiosity won out.

"I had a crazy stalker and got kidnapped but Reid and Eidolon saved me."

"Oh my god, that's awful."

"Yeah, but it was nothing compared to what Taamira went through."

Autumn looked to the Princess who was wearing a deep pink kaftan with gold edging, pale gold trousers that fitted to her ankles, and ballerina pumps.

"We all have stories that start badly. It is why we know how important it is to have friends. You are one of us now, so if you need anything, then we are here for you."

"I don't know what to say." Autumn grinned, the sense of belonging strengthening with every day she spent in the company of these people.

"So, Mitch, huh? He's a handsome devil and such a sweetheart too."

"He's amazing. I don't know what I would've done if I hadn't met him."

Pax looked her dead in the eye. "You would have survived, it's what women like us do."

Autumn returned her gaze, understanding these women were privy to her background and didn't care. She didn't feel the overwhelming urge to hide or run; she felt safe and surrounded by people who understood on a deeper level what she was going through.

"Maybe."

"So, what can we do to help you get sorted?" Taamira glanced at the boxes and then at the baby station. "How about I build that before this little one wakes up?"

"Uh, yes, if you like."

"Callie, you and I can make a start on these boxes of filing while Evelyn goes and sorts lunch." Pax was like a drill sergeant, but in such a way you didn't realise it until it was too late.

"Why do I have to sort lunch?" Evelyn glared at Pax with her hands on her hips and Autumn spied the dynamo beneath the small but sexy exterior.

"Because you can use your wiles on that man of yours to whip us up something nice."

"He's busy on a call."

Pax laughed the sound rich and full. "Use your imagination."

"I'll try." Evelyn closed the door as she left the room.

Callie laughed. "They are so having office sex."

Autumn slapped her hand over her mouth as she tried not to laugh. "No."

Callie nodded. "Oh yeah, this place is a hotbed of sweaty sex when one of us visits. You wouldn't believe how much fun the gym can be when nobody is here." Callie winked, and Autumn's mind went to Mitch, the image of them together filling her head.

Autumn lifted her hand from the desk, wondering if anyone had partaken on there.

"Oh, don't worry, nobody has been in here. This was Ambrose's office. Nobody has used it since he died."

Autumn's belly clenched at Taamira's words. "Someone died?"

"A few years ago, now. He was Jack's second and was killed in an attack. When Alex accepted his role, he took another office because nobody was ready to deal with the fact he was gone."

"I feel awful being in here now. I can move to another space."

Taamira shook her head, her long silky black hair swaying. "No, it is time, and Liam thinks it is a good idea. Ambrose had been his best friend since childhood," she added at Autumn's look of confusion.

She'd no time to ask further questions as Maggie woke up and the room became a hotbed of cooing from the women and shy smiles from Maggie.

Much, much, later, Evelyn came back with plates of brie and apricot chutney sandwiches as well as fruit scones with jam and cream. The women—including Autumn—broke out in laughter when they saw her t-shirt was on backwards, confirming their earlier assumption.

Chapter Fourteen

Mitch wasn't feeling especially talkative on the drive back from Gloucester—the meeting with James Colchester, seventeenth Duke of Crossley and chief legal counsel to the Monarch, hadn't wielded the information they wanted. Now he had to tell Jack who wouldn't be a happy camper.

Thankfully, Decker wasn't much of a talker and left him to his thoughts, most of which involved Autumn. The woman had gotten under his skin far quicker than he'd known, burrowing deep and laying down roots in his heart. Maggie had done the same with her dribbly smiles, and the way she laid her head on his shoulder and snuggled close when she was tired.

Mitch hadn't known that such a simple act of trust could mean so much, but those two females had become his queens, and he'd treat them as such. Protect them with his life because they were his now. It had happened fast, but he'd always known his own mind.

His mother was a strong woman, who had faced every single obstacle thrown in her path with fortitude and dignity. He hated that some of those obstacles had been caused by him, he hadn't realised until he was older how much she'd sacrificed so he'd have a good life.

Moving to a predominantly white, middle-class area had been hard for her. Leaving her friends and everything she knew to start a new life, a new job, had been her gift to him. One he'd always be grateful for, and maybe one day he could repay that. He smiled to himself as he thought of her reaction to Autumn and Maggie. She'd be beside herself with joy when she met them. She was always on at him to give her grandbabies, lamenting she was the only one of her friends without them.

Decker opened the car door as they stopped at Eidolon. "You get on home to Autumn. I can talk to Jack about how the meeting went."

Mitch raised his eyebrows, his eyes going wide. "You sure, mate?"

Decker fiddled with his cuff. "Yes. I have to talk to him about something else anyway."

Mitch nodded. "Cheers, Deck."

Mitch watched Deck walk inside before reversing the car and heading home. Waggs had taken Autumn and Maggie home around five, and he was eager to hear about her first day at work. He hit dial on the steering wheel and waited for his mum to pick up the call. He knew she'd still be up even though it was after nine in the evening, years waiting for him and his step-father to finish a shift meant her habit was ingrained.

"Why are you calling me so late?"

His lips twitched into a grin at her greeting; she always tried to hide her pleasure at hearing from him under her bravado. "Hey, Ma."

"Is everything okay? You don't normally call at this time."

"Can't a boy call his mum just to say hi?"

"Well, of course he can, but you ain't. I can hear it in your voice. You got something to say."

Mitch's grin grew wider as her accent grew more profound; he'd always loved the sound. "I actually do have some news."

"Well, don't keep me waiting, boy. Are you coming home? Is that it?"

He knew she hated him living so far away even though it was only a few hours, but she'd have a fit if she knew what he did. At least she thought he lived away because he had an excellent, safe job with a security firm here.

A chuckle erupted from his throat as a happy feeling clawed its way out of his chest. "No, Ma, I'm not moving back home, but I did meet someone."

"Oh, praise the Lord, my prayers have been answered."

Warmth spread through his chest at the relief in her voice; he hadn't known how much she'd worried about it before.

"What is she like? Is she pretty? Of course she is, my boy is a handsome devil. What does she do? She'd better not be a stripper. I won't have a cheap trollop in my home."

"Ma, will you be quiet and let me tell you about her?"

"Don't you sass me, boy, I'll tan your hide for you."

"Ma," he said, a little more firmly.

"Fine, speak." He heard the smile in her voice even over the irritated words.

"Her name is Autumn. She's a widow and has a baby girl called Maggie, who is six months old and adorable."

"Oh, that poor girl. A baby you say. Does she want more children?"

Mitch shook his head. "I don't know, we haven't discussed it yet. It's still early days."

"But you like her a lot." Her voice went soft and reminded him of the nights she'd come into his room after he'd gone to bed and said the Lord's prayer over him as he feigned sleep.

"I do. I really like her."

"How did you meet?"

That was the question he'd been dreading, and he didn't want to lie to her about it but had no choice. "She's had some trouble, Ma, and my company is helping her out. She's working for us now too."

"I know you'll fix this, my boy. You've always been a fixer. Even as a child, you took a problem or saw someone in need and wanted to help them. I know you wanted to help Devon too, but that boy was already lost."

The words she'd never said before tore at his chest, leaving a lump in his throat. "I think I love her, Mum, and Maggie as well."

"Well, of course you do. You wouldn't get my old heart geared up like this if she wasn't already your heart. When can we meet her?"

"As soon as her problems are sorted out, we'll come down for the weekend."

"Oh, I need to see if Doris has that travel cot... No, forget that, only new for my grandbaby. Send me some pics, baby boy."

"I will. And, Ma, I love you."

"I love you too, my boy, so much."

Mitch hung up then as he pulled into the drive of his home and saw the light still on in Autumn's apartment. He hastened his pace as he walked towards his front door. He made sure to secure it properly before taking the stairs two at a time.

Stopping at her door, he hesitated a second trying to get his body under control, the mere thought of this woman driving him crazy with desire. Sucking in a breath, he blew it out slowly and then knocked, not too loud in case he woke Maggie. He heard the locks disengage on the other side before the chain slid free, then she was standing before him.

His eyes travelled the length of her, from her perfect head to the tips of her toes that were covered in fluffy blue socks. Her legs were bare to his eyes, as she was clad only in sleep shorts and a cotton jersey cami. All his good intentions went out of the window at the sight of her as she smiled, and his heart kicked up a gear.

Without thinking, he pushed inside the apartment, cupping her face between his hands, and kissing her as he backed her up against the wall, closing the door with his booted foot. Autumn's hands moved around his back holding on, a mewling sound of pleasure escaped her as he kissed her like she was his oasis in a dry desert.

He pressed his hard body into her softer one, his hand stroking down her neck, over her collar bone before firmly cupping her lush tit. His thumb rubbed over the tight bud of her nipple, and she squirmed against him, her hands sliding under his shirt so she was touching his skin.

It was heaven and it was hell because he knew he wouldn't take her now, not like this. No, Mitch wanted to take his time, to explore every inch of her sexy body and treat her like the queen she was.

Pulling back, he felt his lips pull into a smile at her moan. She wanted him, and he fucking loved that she did. As his lips moved over the pulse in her neck, he slipped a hand into the tiny shorts she wore and felt the heat of her pussy against his fingers. The slick, wet evidence of her desire for him coating his finger as he entered her, fucking her gently with his two fingers, the sound of her rasping breaths in his ear making his cock impossibly hard.

"You want to come, honey?" Her answer was to push herself into his hand, almost riding his fingers. Mitch pulled back slowly, not allowing her to dictate what was happening. "Answer me with words or I won't let you come. Do you want me to get you off?"

"Yes." The sound was more a moan as he stroked a thumb over the delicate bundle of nerves at her centre, causing her to suck in a sharp breath, her head hitting the wall as she arched into his touch.

He gazed down, in awe of her beauty as he felt her legs begin to shake with her impending orgasm. "You're so fucking beautiful."

His words must have tipped her over the edge because her pussy squeezed his fingers, her breathing became laboured as he covered her mouth with his, drinking in her pleasure as he kissed her.

When she stopped shaking, he slowed his kiss and withdrew his fingers. Lifting his head, he held her eyes with his and licked his fingers, tasting her sweet juices on his tongue. Autumn's eyes were wide and slumberous as she watched, and he knew she liked it by the way she wet her bottom lip with her tongue.

"You taste as sweet as you look."

With a final kiss he pulled away, putting some space between them for a moment but grabbed Autumn's hand, leading her towards the sofa where he sank down with her on his lap. Cradling her with his arms, he waited for her to settle as she drew her legs up and cuddled into him, her head on his shoulder.

"I missed you today."

His admission was unplanned, but it was the truth. He'd never been with a woman he couldn't stop thinking about, but with Autumn, he had no choice. She was on his mind every spare second he had.

"I missed you too and for the record, if that's how you show me you miss me, then you can miss me all the time."

He frowned not liking the idea of missing her, because that meant not being with her. "I don't like that idea. How about I just plan on doing that to you anyway?" His lips twitched as he raised a brow in question. Her husky laughter hit him in the chest, and he wondered if he'd ever get tired of the sound of her happiness and knew he wouldn't.

"That sounds like a plan." Her fingers skimmed over his biceps, the gentle touch almost torture to his aching cock.

"How was your first day at work?" He needed to get his mind off the feel of her body.

"It was good, but not anything like I've experienced before."

"Oh?"

"Well, firstly my office is kitted out with a full range of baby paraphernalia, and then a bunch of women arrived."

"Ah, don't tell me. Pax, Callie, Evelyn, and Taamira?"

"Yes. A model, a Princess, and god knows what Pax and Evelyn are, but they don't work in a bloody Art Gallery."

"They were nice to you?" He felt a sudden overprotectiveness creep in at the thought of her overwhelmed with them all and him not there to intervene.

"They were wonderful, helped me sort the office, built the play centre for Maggie, and caught me up on everything they deemed essential for me to know."

"They're good girls. Actually, I'm glad you met them because there's a party next weekend for a friend of mine. It's at the Cunningham Estate, and everyone is going. Will you come with me?"

He felt nervous as he asked, the beating of his heart faster than before as she laid a hand on his chest, her face falling slightly.

"I can't. I don't have anyone to have Maggie. Not that I'd leave her anyway."

Mitch's tension that had appeared when she'd said she couldn't, eased. "Well, I think I have an idea. The Cunningham Estate is actually a large country home. My friend Zack and his wife own it, and a few families live there, including Nate's parents Mimi and David, and Zack's in-laws Frank and Helen. They usually do childcare after nine at night in a different part of the house from the party. I could ask if they'll look after Maggie too."

Autumn bit her lip and the sexy action made him shift in his seat to relieve the pressure on his dick. "I'm not sure. I haven't left her before, and I don't know these people."

"But you know me, and I'd never ask you to leave Maggie with anyone I don't completely trust."

He saw her hesitate and moved in, lifting her chin so her eyes met his. "I'd never let anyone harm Maggie or you. I just think it would be nice for you to relax and have some fun and for us to do something normal and couple-y. How about this? We go, and if you aren't happy, then we can come home."

"I want that too. I feel like we've skipped the dating stage."

Her soft laughter had guilt moving through him, making him feel like he'd cheated her. Autumn deserved the world, and he'd give it to her one way or another. "I'm sorry, honey. When this is over, I promise to give you all of that, the dates, the fun, but this is a good compromise for now."

"I don't need all that. I actually like that we've skipped over the awkward, uncertain stuff and gone straight to this relaxed intimacy. I don't have time for rubbish like that."

"I've never been more certain of anything in my life than I am of you. In fact, I even told my mother about you tonight."

Autumn straightened, her graceful neck lengthening as her eyes went wide. "You did?"

"Yeah."

"What did she say?"

Mitch scratched his chin. "Well, I wouldn't say she's planning the wedding just yet but she sure as hell is planning the engagement."

Autumn burst out laughing, throwing her head back, exposing the long column of her throat to his lips, which he took full advantage of, nipping at the soft skin before smiling against her neck. "Don't laugh, I'm serious."

"Oh boy, you look worried, Mitch."

Her teasing made him want to kiss her again, this playful side making him fall for her that little bit more. "Not worried, Autumn. If I have my way, you and Maggie will be permanent fixtures in my life."

Her eyes twinkled with warmth as she lifted a hand to cup his face, her thumb brushing over the dark stubble that was littered with more grey than he cared to admit. "How come you stopped earlier?"

He knew what she meant, what she was asking him, and he needed her to know how much he cared about her. He tangled his hands in her long braids, marvelling at the softness. "When I make love to you for the first time, Autumn, it will be in a bed and not one four feet from your daughter. It will be something both of us remember when we're old because I'm going to take my time and discover every inch of your delicious body."

He felt her shiver against him, goosebumps popping up on her skin.

"I want that too, but we don't know when that will be."

Mitch didn't hide the smirk. "Hungry for me, honey?"

Autumn squinted at him, trying to look mad and failing. "Don't be a jerk."

"Sorry, babe, but we both know it's true and I'm just as desperate to feel and taste you. Maybe next weekend we can stay over at the Estate. Some of the rooms are linked, and we could make sure Maggie was within listening distance for us."

"What about after?"

"After, we figure it out, see how this is gonna work for us. Maggie comes first, must always be first in your life, but I want a place in it too."

"I can't believe we're really doing this."

He pushed her hair off her face. "Never met a woman like you before, Autumn. Never thought about settling down but when I saw you it was like looking at my future. The second I met you, I knew you'd change my life."

"Is it wrong that I feel the same? It feels almost like a betrayal. Terrell wasn't always bad. He was a good man in the beginning, he just got lost."

His heart sped up at her words. "He must've been a good man once because I refuse to believe that a woman like you could love anyone not worthy of her. Let me ask you something. If he were still alive, would you be with him now?"

Autumn looked up, giving his words thought, which he respected. "No, I wouldn't. He made his choice, and I'd never allow him to put me and Maggie second. I don't want my daughter to ever feel like she's second best. It already hurts my heart to know that one day I'll have to explain to her why people judge her for how she looks, for the colour of her skin."

Mitch had suffered his fair share of racism, it was impossible not to and the scars it left were always with him, would still be with him when he was old and grey. This town had very few people of colour, plenty of people from Eastern Europe but to see a black man or woman was rare here. Yet he didn't receive the same hostility from some that he'd had in London.

Furtive looks, and even some ignorance, but not once since living here had he been attacked for the colour of his skin. The worst he'd had was Mrs Mullins asking if he knew the lovely coloured family that lived on West Street.

He'd told her no and asked if she knew the people that lived in Sommerset House. She'd blinked and said no, and then understanding had dawned in the canny older woman's eyes and she'd apologised.

That he could live with, ignorance from people who were willing to learn and change was okay with him. He didn't profess to know about every different culture, but he'd always try and learn, and if others did the same, understanding his struggle as a black man, then he was happy with that.

As he saw the fear in Autumn's eyes, he remembered the times he'd seen it in his mother's eyes. "We'll make sure Maggie is strong enough to deal with whatever she may face, and she'll know we're behind her whatever that may be."

"I haven't been subjected to any racism here yet."

"No, I haven't had a lot either. Hereford isn't London, thank goodness. Yes, you get some people who are stuck up their own ass and look at you differently but not in my circle of friends."

"I'm glad I ended up here."

"Me too, beautiful, me too."

Mitch stayed the night, lying on the bed next to her on top of the covers so he wasn't tempted to break his own rules. Autumn was too important to rush, she and Maggie were his happy ever after, even though he'd be a fool to believe in that after the horrors he'd seen, he'd also seen the best of people and it gave him hope.

Chapter Fifteen

Autumn hit send on the final email of the day to Alex and sat back in her chair. This week had been exhausting but in a good way. She felt accomplished intellectually for the first time in over a year. The work had been very different from what she was used to but no less challenging.

She'd been surprised by how much went into an operation such as this. It had been eye-opening, allowing her to truly appreciate the sacrifices these men made with no recognition or thanks from the people or countries they worked for. They did get paid an eye-watering amount though and being party to that knowledge made her feel a little guilty.

Terrell had always been jealous that she got paid more than him, old fashioned in his thinking regarding finances and family. Autumn snorted a laugh at the thought he could be so traditional in his thinking about money but had then helped a psycho like Linton Allen build chemical weapons.

It had taken her a while to get her head around that, but she knew in her heart that what Eidolon suspected was probably right. Pushing her chair back, she crossed to the corner and looked at her sleeping daughter, hoping she'd sleep tonight. Bebe and Aubrey were coming around to help her decide what to wear tomorrow night. It had been years since she'd had any kind of girl's night, probably not since her days in the dorms at Uni.

Hearing a cheering sound, she moved out of her office, closing the door and taking the baby monitor so she could still listen for Maggie and followed the sound which got louder as she walked towards the gym. It was a full house today with all the Eidolon men in for some sort of strategy session she wasn't privy to.

Rounding the corner, she stopped, a small gasp escaping her as she saw all of the guys standing around the training ring in the middle of the room dressed in workout gear. Her eyes were focused solely on the man in the middle of the ring, though.

Mitch stood facing Reid in the centre. His naked chest glistened with sweat, the muscles of his pecs bunching and flexing as he danced around the other man, his fists up in front of his face.

Autumn felt the spit in her mouth dry out at the sight of such a beautiful specimen. Reid was hot too, with his tattoos and bad boy vibe, but Mitch personified male beauty to her. The sleek muscles, the sheen of his umber-brown skin had her wanting to feel him under her hands.

Without realising it, she moved forward, drawn to the brutality as the two men fought and they didn't hold back. Each landing blow after blow, as they punched and blocked, their skill levels perfectly matched.

She came to a stop beside Waggs who was watching so intently she almost jumped when he spoke.

"Part of fighting is learning how to take a hit. It's why we never hold back in the ring." His arms crossed over his chest as he leaned sideways to speak to her before casting her an unreadable glance.

"Do they do this often?" Her voice held the barest hint of the shock she felt.

"We all do. Eidolon can't afford to have weak men."

"Who normally wins?"

"Depends on the fight. If it's boxing like they're doing now," he pointed at Reid, who had just taken a punch to the face from Mitch, and was shaking it off like a dog shaking water off his body, "then normally Mitch. If it's more Jujitsu stuff, Blake wins. MMA would be Reid, and street fighting is Liam's thing. But Jack always beats us at all of them."

Autumn glanced at Jack, who was walking the perimeter of the ring, arms folded as he observed his men. "How and why?"

"Jack is the boss, and he believes in order to be a good leader, he should be able to do what we do only better, so he makes it happen."

"Wow, I guess this is another world I had no clue about."

"You're doing great, Autumn. You're Lopez's hero right now."

Autumn chuckled, and at the sound, Mitch turned to catch her eye, catching a punch to the ribs in the distracted second.

"Ouch." Autumn winced as the men groaned. "I should probably go. I don't want him hurt because of me."

Waggs regarded her with a look she couldn't read before he nodded, a tiny smile twitching on his serious face.

Autumn backed out, heading for her office, a thrill coursing through her at the sight of Mitch in such a different light to the one she knew. Violence had never appealed to her, but she'd be lying if she denied seeing him like that hadn't turned her on, but then Mitch had that effect on her. Making her feel needy and wanton with his kisses and hands but never letting her return the favour no matter how much she wanted it.

Part of her respected that he cared so much about their first time, but she was ready to know what it felt like to be possessed by a man like him. Seeing the edge of darkness he hid only thrilled her more, maybe because no matter what, she always felt safe with him. More than that, she felt like a queen, and he treated Maggie with the same love and tenderness.

It was easy to forget the threat she still faced when surrounded by so much support and protection. Yet it was always there, that anxiety that Allen would get to her now he'd technically found her and rip this beautiful life she was building away from her.

Mitch assured her that Allen was always under watch now and they'd know if he made any moves towards her. It gave her some comfort as she lifted a now wide-eyed Maggie from her crib.

"Are you ready for your first girl's night, Roo?"

In the past, she'd felt slightly daft talking to Maggie, but now she smiled as she remembered hearing Mitch do the same thing just the other night.

Packing up her stuff, she heard the commotion as the men filtered in from the gym towards the showers. Her spine prickled with awareness the second Mitch stepped inside the room.

She turned, her eyes roving over his body in a slow appraisal, mourning the fact he'd donned a shirt. Her eyes flashed back to his face as she took in the split lip. She was moving towards him before she knew it. "Your lip?" Autumn touched the swollen lip with her fingertips.

His hand grasped her wrist, and she saw the reflected desire in his eyes. "It's nothing."

"Did you win?"

Mitch shook his head. "Not this time. I got distracted by a beautiful woman, then all I could think about was her." His grin told her he wasn't mad by it.

Maggie leaned out of her arms towards Mitch, who took her but held her away from his body as he dropped a kiss on her head. "I'm all sweaty, gorgeous."

Maggie didn't care and babbled at him, making them both laugh.

"Are you excited about your evening?"

Autumn nodded. "I am, but it will seem strange you being across the hall instead of on my sofa."

Mitch chuckled. "Believe me, if I were there for a girl's night, I'd be shown the door in short order. Plus, I have to go get my hair cut at the barber's shop later." He rubbed a hand over his hair that didn't look like it needed a cut to her.

"Who does it? I need to find a hairdresser who knows how to do box braids and soon. Before the growth gets in a mess."

"A guy called Sam on Bridge Street has a barber's shop. His wife does braids and weaves."

Autumn pursed her lip. "Do you think she could fit me in tomorrow?"

"I'll find out, but I'm sure they can. Do you need me to watch Maggie while you have it done?"

"Would you?"

"Of course, although you'll need someone to stay with you at the salon. I won't have you there alone."

"Do you think Bebe or Aubrey would?" Aubrey was police and she knew Bebe was in security although she was still a little unsure what she did. Having worked for Eidolon for only a week, she'd quickly realised that all was not as it seemed at Zenobi's Art Gallery.

"Ask them tonight."

Autumn looked at her watch, suddenly realising the time. "Oh shit, I need to go."

Mitch handed Maggie back to her. "Let me take a real quick shower, and we'll head home."

Autumn's heart skipped as he used the word home. Such a simple word and yet one she hadn't felt for a long time.

---

* * *

Bebe laid around ten outfits on hangers over the back of Autumn's couch. "So, I've brought over a few options as I know you probably don't have a huge amount of party dresses."

94

She was right, shopping and clothes had ceased to be meaningful the moment she'd seen her husband murdered. "That's so kind of you."

Bebe waved a hand. "I have too many clothes. I think we're about the same size and I brought some pumps too. You're a size six, right?"

Autumn nodded as she moved to let Aubrey in, who hugged and kissed her as if she were her long lost sister.

"I have wine." She shook the bottle lightly, and Autumn grinned, her shoulders relaxing. Taking the wine, she opened it and poured three glasses as Aubrey shucked her denim jacket. "Is Maggie asleep?"

Autumn shook her head. "No, Mitch took her over to his apartment for an hour so I could tidy up and make us some nibbles."

Aubrey's face softened. "That's so sweet."

"He's amazing with her," Autumn agreed as she handed them each a glass.

"So, it's going well then?" Bebe asked with a cheeky wiggle of her eyebrows.

"It is, which shocks me."

Aubrey inclined her head. "Why?"

"I never thought I'd have this again. I was all set to live my life alone, just me and Maggie, and now I have a man who treats me like a goddess and friends who accept me for who I am." Autumn took a sip of her wine, the sharp, sweet tang hitting her taste buds. "I guess it's all just hard to get my head around."

Aubrey laid a hand over hers as she sat beside her on the couch. "You've been through a lot. It's easy to understand how you might feel that way, but let me tell you from someone who has known him a little while now, Mitch is a good guy, one of the best, and he adores you and Maggie."

Bebe nodded. "Yep, a few hearts broke when you bagged that man."

Autumn laughed a light-hearted feeling in her chest.

The door opened and Mitch walked in with Maggie in his arms, Will behind him. "This little angel is ready for her bed and she needs a feed."

He moved across the living room and handed Maggie into her outstretched arms. He'd changed her into a yellow onesie with blue rabbits on it, and Maggie was already looking sleepy.

"Thanks for getting her changed."

Mitch leaned down, bracing his hands either side of her on the sofa. "My pleasure." He kissed her quickly before pulling back to look at her, totally ignoring the heat on her cheeks or the sighs from the women beside her. "Simone, Sam's wife, can fit you in tomorrow at noon if you still want to get your hair done."

Autumn bit her lip and looked at Aubrey and Bebe. "Any chance you want to come with me while I get my hair done? I need a babysitter for Maggie and me." She shrugged. "Maggie got Mitch."

"Yes, of course. I need to get my nails done anyway," Bebe readily agreed.

"I'm working until two, but Will can go with you both."

Aubrey shot her man a grin, and he gave her a frown before groaning. "Fine, but I'm bringing my laptop."

Aubrey grinned at Autumn. "He loves it really."

Mitch and Will left then, but not before Will claimed a kiss from Aubrey and Mitch laid another kiss on her and Maggie.

"Make yourselves at home while I just give her a quick feed and put her down. I won't be long."

Autumn escaped the stares from the two women who were becoming her friends. Having been on her own for so long it was hard to let people into such a private part of her life, but she wanted to be the old her again.

Taking the time to feed Maggie and set her down quietly gave her the peace she needed to go and face her new friends.

Going back into the living room, she smiled at the two women as she twisted her hair around her finger in a show of nerves. It was one thing people knowing about her and Mitch but showing them was different.

"We scared you off," Bebe announced as Autumn walked towards the kitchen and began pulling food from the fridge.

"No, not at all." She popped the tray of mango chicken lollipops and plantain puff puffs in the oven to cook before looking at Bebe. "I was always affectionate with my family but Terrell, my husband, hated PDA, thought it was embarrassing, so I think I got out of practice. Does that make sense? I got into a habit of hiding my feelings in public, and it's a hard mindset to break."

"It does, but I have a feeling Mitch is into public displays of affection." Aubrey scowled at Bebe who laughed. "Not in a freaky let's get it on in public kind of way, although…" She smiled as Aubrey threw a cushion at her.

"Shut up. You're going to scare her off, dumbass." Aubrey frowned but her eyes were smiling.

"Let's see what outfits you've brought over," Autumn said, changing the subject.

Aubrey gave her a wink and Bebe came around the sofa and started lifting hangers.

"This would look fabulous on you."

She handed Autumn a purple dress with a high neck and long sleeves which would fit like a second skin and fall to her knee. Autumn wrinkled her nose as she imagined the fabric around her neck. "I don't like anything around my neck."

"What about this one?" Aubrey asked, handing her a cerise pink dress, with a black lace bodice. It was short, probably only falling to her mid-thigh, but it was beautiful.

"Oh yes, go try it on," Bebe ordered.

With a happy feeling, Autumn went into the bathroom and slid the dress on. It was skintight on her but hugged the curves of her ass, accentuating her small waist thanks to baby Pilates. Turning, she realised a bra wouldn't work as it was too revealing. It was beautiful, and she felt sexy in it, her boobs shouldn't leak either because she'd started weaning Maggie now.

"Get your ass out here," Bebe called from the closed door.

Autumn opened the door, and Bebe whistled.

"Wow, you're gonna knock Mitch on his ass in that dress."

"Show me," Aubrey said from the kitchen where she was checking the chicken in the oven. Her expression went wide. "You look spectacular. You have amazing legs."

Autumn laughed, courage warming through her at the words. These two women and the ones she'd met on Monday were already imbuing her with confidence, and it was a feeling she hadn't realised she'd lost until she felt the first twinges as it came back.

Chapter Sixteen

Mitch opened the car door and leaned in to lift Maggie's car seat out. Autumn walked towards her, her eyes on the big house in front of them full of trepidation.

"Don't look so nervous." He laid a hand on the small of her back as he ushered her towards the large double front door, which was opening.

Ava was smiling at them, a welcome expression on her face which he appreciated.

"What if they don't like me?" Autumn whispered out of the side of her mouth.

His shoulders tensed at the worry in her words. He forced them to relax and pulled her close, his hand sliding into the back pocket of the jeans she wore. "How could anyone not like you? You're beautiful and funny and sweet."

Autumn turned her eyes to him and raised a delicate brow. "Flatterer."

Mitch winked. "Truth, baby."

Ava stepped back as she greeted them. "It is so lovely to meet you. I have to say it's so exciting to meet the woman who's responsible for wrangling Eidolon's office into submission."

Autumn laughed. "I wouldn't go so far as to say submission, but we are making progress."

Mitch angled her way. "Nonsense, the place is already running more smoothly."

Autumn dropped her gaze at the compliment, and it made him want to punch the person who'd made her doubt herself. She was everything—kind, smart, beautiful, and yet she didn't seem to get that. It made him rage inside that it might be someone he'd grown up with that had started this self-doubt.

"And who is this little angel?" Ava crouched down and took Maggie's hand with a smile.

"This is Maggie."

Ava looked up with warmth in her eyes. "What a beautiful name for a beautiful baby." Her voice had taken on the sing-song quality that most people did when they talked to a child.

"Thank you."

Mitch could feel Autumn relax a little as Ava showed them to the room they'd share tonight.

Her wide eyes took in the large suite as she walked to the window, much like she had the day she'd come to look at the flat. It felt like a lifetime ago, and yet like it was yesterday. It was hard to imagine what his life had been like without these two females who were winding themselves around his heart like a vine.

"Wow, this is gorgeous." She turned to him. "Can we explore the gardens before we get ready?"

Mitch wasn't sure what she needed to do to get ready. She looked amazing in fresh box braids twisted into a bun on top of her head, her face beautiful without a spec of make-up on.

"Sure, we have time."

Her face lit up, and his heart constricted as she moved to lace her arms around his waist and reach up to kiss him. Mitch deepened the kiss for a moment, loving the taste of her and the way she leaned into him, before pulling away. The heavy bead of desire hung in her dark eyes, and his body responded.

"You're dangerous." His eyes held hers as he tried to push the tingle of fear at losing her away.

"Why?" Her lips quirked, and she frowned.

"Because you can wind me around your little finger with just a look, and I haven't even been inside you yet."

"Oh."

He pressed his lips to her neck, chuckling against her skin. "Yeah, oh."

A cry tore his focus from the woman in his arms, and he looked down at Maggie

"How about we go meet Mimi and David and the others who'll be taking care of this little one? They're also the resident gardening committee here, so you can talk plants and weeds to your heart's content with someone who doesn't zone out from boredom."

He smirked at her outraged expression. "Jerk." Her words held no heat as she batted his arm.

"Hey, I'm injured." He pointed to his lip which was now only showing a small cut.

Her nose wrinkled, eyes smiling. "I guess we should probably put off tonight's plans then." Her coy smile flittered over her face, and he loved the natural teasing between them.

He cupped her neck. "Not a fucking chance. Tonight, I'm going to taste every delicious inch of this body." His finger skirted over the side curve of her breast, and she shivered, causing him to smile triumphantly. His lips moved to her ear. "Then I'm going to bury my cock inside you until I find every sweet spot you have and make you breathless as you cry my name."

Her throat moved as she swallowed, and he released her to stumble back a step.

Bending, he lifted Maggie from her car seat then turned to Autumn. "Ready?" His words had a double meaning, and he knew she knew it.

"So ready."

Her answer pleased him, and he kissed her temple in approval before leading her to the door.

* * *

Mitch had left Autumn to get ready and taken Maggie to the other side of the house where Mimi, David, and the others would be looking after the kids. They had all fallen completely in love with Autumn, and when she'd started talking gardening, they were goners, just as he was.

Every second he spent with her cemented his growing feelings for the woman who'd blown into his ordered life like a storm and cleared away any doubt about what he wanted in his future, and that was her and Maggie.

He frowned as he saw Jack striding towards him. He was already dressed for the party Zin was throwing for his girlfriend Celeste in black trousers and a black shirt open at the neck, but Jack's eyes were hard as ice.

"What happened?"

"Just got word Autumn's previous handler was the one who gave her up."

"Fuck," Mitch exclaimed savagely and regretted it as Maggie flinched in his arms. His hand came out to cup her head as he kissed her temple. "Sorry, baby, I didn't mean to scare you." He looked back at Jack. "Let me take Maggie into Mimi and then we can talk."

Jack nodded and walked with him, waiting and chatting with Frank.

Mitch settled Maggie and gave Mimi the instructions she needed even as she smiled at him like he was an idiot. "Milk is in the bag. She'll have a bottle at ten and then she should sleep through until around four, but we'll have her by then."

The older woman who'd beaten Kanan, a fearless ex-MI5 spy, with a welsh cake griddle patted his hand in a gentle way he recognised because his mum was the same. "I know how to suck eggs, dear boy."

Mitch barked a laugh and kissed her head. "I know Mimi, but Autumn is nervous. She's never been away from Maggie before and this is a big deal for her."

Her eyes softened. "I'll look after her as if she were my own."

Mitch nodded, knowing she'd do just that.

Out in the hallway, he walked with Jack to the end of the hall to find them some privacy.

"What else?"

Jack looked like he'd chewed a wasp. "We caught Hench going into Autumn's parent's house before leaving fifteen minutes later with Autumn's younger brother. That was two hours ago."

Mitch felt anger swirl through him; it was a low tactic, and one they should've expected.

"Where's Rion now?" It hadn't taken a lot of work for Lopez to find her entire family's details and Rion had slipped further off the straight and narrow since his sister had left.

"He returned home, but Will found this on the dark web just before we left."

Jack showed Mitch an image of Hench with Autumn's parents and brother in what he assumed was their living room. That was terrifying enough, but the caption underneath was meant for Mitch.

Stop being a coward and face me, or your girlfriend will lose more than her family.

Mitch looked at Jack, anger and fear burning through him at what this would do to Autumn.

"I'm gonna kill him."

"We have him, Hench, and Midas under surveillance now. We need to get into the warehouse and end this."

"Agreed."

He looked up, and Jack followed his gaze. Mitch felt the air leave him at the vision of perfection in front of him.

Jack laid a hand on his arm. "Take tonight, and we'll follow this up in the morning."

Mitch nodded but couldn't take his eyes off Autumn. She wore a bright pink dress that clung to her body like a glove, the hem hitting mid-thigh, the silk sheen of her muscular thighs making his mouth water. His eyes travelled up over her curved hips, small waist, to lush breasts encased in the black lace bodice of the dress.

He heard a chuckle beside him and dragged his gaze away for a second as he saw Liam and Taamira heading towards the ballroom where he realised music had begun to play. Ignoring the knowing grin on Liam's face, he looked back to Autumn who was nearly to him. She'd applied make-up that made her look like a siren, full pink lips covered in gloss, with long dark lashes.

Holding her hands at hip level palm up, she turned a grin on her face. "Well?"

Mitch growled, everything else falling away as he grasped her, pulling her to his body. "You make me want to hide you away. Every single man in the room is going to be imagining you naked when they see you."

"Well, only one gets to."

With his arm firmly around her, he kissed the spot just below her ear, feeling the full-body shiver before he led her towards the ballroom. He saw Alex and Evelyn with Liam and Taamira and nodded as he headed to the bar. "What would you like to drink?"

"Can I get a vodka and cranberry?"

Mitch ordered it for her and a beer for himself. He had every intention of fucking her tonight and wanted to be sober when he did it. He handed her the drink before moving through the bar. He introduced her to Dane, who was Zack's second and his wife Lauren. Then Daniel and Meg, who was also a scientist and before long, the two women were talking about compounds and formulas like best friends.

Mitch turned to Daniel. "Does anyone know why he's throwing this party?"

Daniel shrugged. "It's her birthday next month so we figured that, although I think Roz and Skye might know more. It's been a nightmare keeping this from her though."

Mitch raised his brows. "She doesn't know anything?"

Celeste had a very rare gift; she could read peoples thoughts and feelings through touch.

Daniel nodded. "No. Do you know how hard it was keeping it from her? It's okay for Zin, he can block it somehow, but the rest of us have been avoiding her like the plague in case she accidentally brushes an arm or hand."

"I guess you're all still frightened of Zin?"

Mitch was joking, nobody was scared of Zin as such but he was a deadly bastard with a knack for torture.

"Okay, everyone, quiet down. They're pulling up," Skye said, waving her hands as Roz just glared them all into silence.

The doors were closed, and the room fell silent. Autumn looked at him and lifted her shoulders as she grinned at the drama of it all, excitement evident in her face. They could hear murmuring and then the door swung open and Celeste stopped dead, her hands slapping to her cheeks as she looked from them to Zin and back again.

"Surprise," they all called out.

Celeste looked like a rabbit caught in the headlights as Zin ushered her into the middle of the room. As she turned back to Zin, a gasp rang through the room, not just from Celeste but from every female in the room.

"Pixie, I've loved you since the day I met you. My life meant nothing without you in it and now you *are* my life. The air I breathe, the life running through my veins belongs to you. Will you please be my wife and let me love you into eternity?" He was down on one knee, an open velvet box in his hands and looking more terrified than Mitch had ever seen.

He heard a sigh beside him and Autumn leaned into him with a sniffle as Celeste threw her arms around Zin, knocking him to the floor.

"Yes."

A cheer went up, but Mitch doubted Celeste or Zin heard, too caught up in the moment.

Autumn touched her heart. "That was so beautiful."

"I think she'd given up hope of him asking, they've been together a while."

"I guess he wanted the timing to be right," Meg said.

"Or he was scared stiff of the commitment?" Daniel parried as he put his arm around Meg and kissed her soundly.

"Don't you spoil my fun."

Daniel nuzzled her neck and whispered in her ear, causing Meg to blush beet red.

Usher's DJ Got Us Fallin' In Love Again began to play. "Dance?"

Autumn nodded. Taking her hand, Mitch pulled her to the middle of the dancefloor, and they began to move to the music. Watching her body move as she relaxed and let the music move through her was pleasure and pain. He wanted her so badly he could taste it, but more than that, he loved seeing the unabashed joy on her face as she laughed.

"You've got moves, Mr Quinn."

"You sound shocked."

"Well, you are getting up there in age."

Her teasing made him chuckle as he snagged her waist. "You're gonna pay for that later, Ms Roberts."

Her laughter in his ear was his only response as she draped her arms around his neck and danced against him, her hips brushing his cock, making him groan.

As their friends danced around them, he relaxed knowing the company they were in understood what it was to let go when you had to stay so focused in everyday life with the danger they faced.

As Autumn leaned into him, putting her whole trust in him, his heart felt light as he also realised he'd fallen in love with the woman in his arms. They stayed that way until she lifted her head, eyes bright with joy.

"We should get a drink, I'm parched."

Mitch grinned at her proper English and kissed her, enjoying the way she wound her arms around his neck. Pulling back he took her hand and led her from the dance floor towards the bar.

As the moved through his friends he saw Zin and Celeste and stopped to congratulate the couple who looked beyond happy.

He shook the big Russians hand firmly. "You're a lucky man, Zin."

"Thank you. Yes, I'm the luckiest man in the world to have my Pixie."

Mitch looked down at Autumn as she cuddled into him. "I think this room is full of couples that feel that way. We're the lucky ones."

"Yes.   Yes,   we   are."

Chapter Seventeen

Her feet ached from dancing, her jaw from smiling but Autumn was happier than she'd been—ever—not including the day she'd given birth to her beautiful Roo who she'd checked on twice and found sleeping as the older couples played cards.

Mitch had come with her the first time she checked, but the second, he'd lifted his head for a kiss first, and she'd willingly given it to him. After her reservations the other day, it had come naturally to show him affection, her true nature kicking in. Seeing the other couples who were all openly tactile and loving had helped her relax.

They were sitting at a table with Daniel, Meg, Reid, Callie, Kanan, and Roz, the latter slightly terrifying in her opinion. Mitch had his arm around the back of her chair, his thumb stroking over the skin just above the lace of her dress, making her pulse quicken.

"You ready to call it a night or do you want to dance some more?" Mitch's eyes were swimming with erotic promise, but he was giving her a choice.

Autumn felt the ache of desire pool between her legs. "Bed." It was the only word she got out before he was standing, and they were saying goodnight to the others at the table.

"Give me a call if you ever want to get back into science," Meg said before hugging her tight.

"I will, thank you."

Mitch laid his hand at the base of her spine as he walked out with her. "Do you want to get Maggie and get her settled or have you decided to take Mimi up on her offer?"

Autumn twisted her fingers nervously. "I just don't think I can leave her. They're lovely but..."

His fingers against her lips stopped her words. "You don't have to explain why you don't want to leave your baby overnight. If you want her, we'll get her, and she sleeps in our suite."

Autumn felt her body relax but still wanted to ask. "Are you mad?"

Mitch frowned as they walked to the other side of the enormous house. "Why would I be mad?"

"Well, you planned to, you know."

Mitch chuckled and bent close to her ear. "Oh, I still plan to, we just have to be more creative."

His lips brushed her pulse as they reached the door and she had no time to respond or get her own body under control before he was thanking Mimi and David and lifting a sleeping Maggie from her crib.

Autumn thanked the older couples and promised to visit again soon, all while her mind was on the sensual promise Mitch had made.

Once back in the suite, her eyes flew to the large bed, and her body trembled with anticipation. "Do you want me to settle Maggie while you do whatever it is women do before bed?"

Autumn laughed her shoulders relaxing. "It's fine. I can just give her a dream feed and then she won't wake."

Mitch looked perplexed. "A dream feed?"

"Yeah, it's a feed where the baby pretty much stays asleep through it."

Mitch nodded and followed her into the bedroom where the crib was set up. It was a smaller room than the one they shared and had the bathroom in between. Autumn felt happy with that though because she was still close to Maggie and had the monitor set up by the bed. Mitch handed Maggie over and kissed her head before leaving them.

Autumn quickly got Maggie settled in the bed, taking a moment to stroke her cheek before taking a steadying breath and walking into the bedroom. Her nerves had made another appearance, all the self-doubt about her body rearing its ugly head. The last man she'd slept with, in fact, the only man, had been her husband and she'd changed a lot physically since then.

Mitch was sitting on the edge of the bed watching her. He'd removed his shoes and socks, and something about seeing his bare feet felt intimate to her.

Tilting his head to the side, he held out a hand to her. "Come here, honey."

Autumn walked towards him. His eyes were liquid with desire as she took his hand and he drew her between his muscular thighs, the tease of his rough hands on her hips burning with heat through the fabric of the dress.

"Nervous?" he asked as he placed delicate kisses on her wrist to her elbow.

"A little." Autumn's pulse danced in her neck as her breasts heaved with need.

"We can stop whenever you want, okay."

Autumn shook her head. "No, I want this. You. But it's been a while."

His hand stole over the curve of her ass as he twisted, pulling her down to the bed, so she lay beneath his hard body.

"So soft, your skin is like satin."

The light beside the bed cast a warm glow over his features, the proud angle of his jaw sharp with masculine beauty.

Reaching up, she pulled his mouth down to her own, seeking out his tongue with her own, confidence growing at his soft words.

Mitch took over, his hands stroking her skin, driving her need higher, her skin tingling from every touch.

Mitch pulled back, his eyes on hers. His hand went to the side of her dress, the hiss of the zipper mingling with the sounds of their breathing. His fingertips skimmed her, and she arched into his touch, shifting her legs to ease the ache in her pussy. She felt empty, wanted to feel him inside her.

Her hand stole down his toned stomach to where she could feel his heavy cock against her inner thigh. Wrapping her hand around him, she squeezed, enjoying the heady power as he groaned. Pulling the dress down over her arms as she worked his cock through his trousers, Mitch sucked a pebbled nipple into his mouth. The sensitive nub and the bite of his teeth made her arch her back off the bed, her other hand holding his head where she wanted him.

His eyes rose to hers, and she stared at the sight of this powerful man giving her pleasure. Releasing her nipple with a pop, he kissed his way down her belly, taking the dress over her hips before lifting her legs to throw it behind him.

Kneeling between her legs, he lifted his arms, the sinew and muscle of his biceps rippling as he tore his shirt over his head. Autumn's mouth went dry at his beauty, his skin glistened with a sheen of sweat, the ridges of his six-pack and pecs making her mouth water.

Gliding his hands over her thighs, he cupped the globes of her ass before hooking the underside of her black lace thong and pulling it slowly down her legs, tossing it to the floor beside her dress.

Autumn stretched her arms above her head feeling free and cherished, her confidence growing with every look.

"Let's see if you taste as good as you look."

Mitch buried his face in her pussy, his tongue licking her from front to back, finding her entrance and lapping at her desire like a starved man. His eyes still on her he sucked the nub of her clit into his mouth as his fingers moved inside her stroking and massaging her secret spot, unravelling her tension as her climax built. She was so wet with arousal any other time she would've felt heat flooding her face, but she was too lost, too caught up in the race for her orgasm.

Autumn's legs began to shake, her hand landing on his head, as the other gripped the silk pillow and held it to her mouth to silence her scream of release. Arching her back, she splintered in ecstasy, shards of bright light blinking in her vision as her climax thundered through her body, every nerve pulsing with pleasure such as she'd never known before.

She felt the pillow pulled from her face as a now naked Mitch stood magnificently between her legs, his sheathed cock in his hand as he pumped the thick shaft.

"I could live on the taste of you on my lips." His erotic words had her body throbbing with arousal again, her muscles languid from it. "You're like a dream I can hardly believe is real, but here you are spread out like a banquet, and I want to taste every inch of your skin."

Autumn held hands up to him, Mitch complied, resting his weight on her, his hands either side of her head, hips cradled between her thighs. The heat of his erection twitched against her entrance.

"I want to feel you inside me."

Her mouth found his and Mitch kissed her as he slid inside her, the burn of the stretch mixing with desire, heightening her senses. When he was entirely inside her, he kissed her tenderly, before his hips began to move, his cock pumping inside her as she wrapped her legs around his back, locking him to her. Rocking up to meet every pump of his hips, her moans fought with the sound of slapping flesh, his scent surrounding her adding to her desire.

Mitch pulled away, the feral look in his eyes only making her wetter, her nails digging into the strength of his shoulders as she buried her head in his neck and bit down, her climax taking her over the edge.

Mitch shook as his pelvis slammed into her, and she tightened around him as he swelled and pulsed, releasing his seed into the latex between them as his climax barrelled through him and he sought her mouth.

Her eyes opened, and he was watching her with a possessive look in his eyes as he stroked her cheek with his thumb.

"You're mine."

Autumn shivered at his words, feeling claimed in a way her husband had never made her feel. Mitch owned her body and mind, and the thought was both terrifying and exhilarating.

As he withdrew from her she winced at the movement, her body aching in places she'd forgotten she had.

Mitch froze, his brow dipping in concern. "Did I hurt you?"

Autumn shook her head. "No, I'm just not used to it."

Mitch nodded, his eyes devouring her as she lay shamelessly naked on the mint green silk bedding. His finger skimmed her hip as he stepped away from the bed, the hair on his legs tickling her skin.

Autumn stared as he prowled to the bathroom, his fine ass making her spent body awaken with renewed energy. The front was no less spectacular as he ambled towards her, his cock still half erect. He was a magnificent specimen, and she found herself smiling that she could call him hers.

"What you grinning at?" He climbed on the bed beside her, lying on his side, his head resting in his hand, his elbow propped and laid his palm on her belly, his eyes intent.

"Just how sexy you are."

"Oh yeah?"

Autumn pushed up, rolling so he was on his back, Mitch letting her take control. Her breasts pressed into the hair on his chest smattered with hints of grey, only making him sexier in her eyes. Her hands moved over his belly, following the trail of hair towards his cock which lay semi-erect against his muscular thigh.

110

"I'm not sure if I mentioned this, but I'm not a teenager anymore. Two in a row is a bit of an ask." His chuckle made her belly squirm, the feel of his body under her hands, causing her clit to pulse.

"Is that a challenge?" Her voice was a purr she couldn't remember hearing before, a seductive tone only for him.

"If you want it to be."

Autumn laughed a throaty sound and saw his dick twitch as she kissed her way down his belly and took the tip of him into her mouth. His deep hiss of pleasure, the feel of his rough hand stroking the curve of her ass before sliding into the wetness at her centre, made her take more of his already hard cock into her mouth. Hollowing her cheeks, she sucked, taking him deeper as he pumped his fingers into her.

Soon she tasted the evidence of his desire sharp on her tongue and knew she wanted it all. Her hands caressed his balls as she hummed around his cock, making him jerk his hips.

"Fuck me, Autumn, that's so good."

Smiling around his dick, she redoubled her efforts as Mitch hooked his fingers inside her, rubbing his thumb over her clit, in circular motions until they were both writhing.

"Autumn."

His warning threw her over the edge, and she climaxed around his fingers as she swallowed his length, the first jets of his seed hitting her throat. Letting his cock fall from her lips, Autumn collapsed on his belly.

"I think I died and went to heaven."

Autumn shot him a glare. "No dying. I only just found you."

Mitch held his arms out to her and she crawled up him, cuddling into his body in the space he left for her.

Draping his arm over her hip, he pulled her tighter against him. "I'm not going anywhere, Autumn. I never had a reason like you and Maggie to live for before, and I was careful, but now I'll do whatever it takes to makes sure you and she are safe and that I always come home to you."

The three little words hung on her tongue, but she bit them back, not wanting it to feel like a cliché after they'd just made love. Yet in her heart, she knew she loved this man with everything in her and his

111

words, although not love, made her think he felt the same. She trusted him to keep her heart and that of her precious baby girl safe.

Chapter Eighteen

Mitch woke early and glanced at the beauty beside him. He wanted to roll over and wake her with his mouth, but he could hear Maggie cooing to herself in the other room. Sliding out from under the arm that was slung possessively over his belly, he leaned in to kiss her bare shoulder. Autumn lay on her front, the sheet pooled around her hips, the expanse of sexy flesh teasing him.

He rubbed a hand over his face then slid his legs into jeans and donned a tee before padding into the room where Maggie had slept. He looked down at her and grinned as she shoved her foot in her mouth.

"How about we get you some breakfast, gorgeous." He reached in and scooped her up, feeling the weight of a very wet nappy. "Perhaps we should get you dressed first."

He'd done this a few times under Autumn's careful tutelage, and after finding everything he needed, he got Maggie dressed in the cutest little denim pinafore dress.

With a glance at Autumn, he wondered about leaving a note, but she'd know he had Maggie and that he'd bring coffee back for her. Taking the stairs, he followed the noise to the large kitchen where Mimi and Alex were making breakfast.

"Morning!" Mimi greeted with a smile.

Alex cast his eye over him and then smirked a knowing grin.

"Mimi, Alex, good morning."

"Did you sleep well?" she asked as she flipped a piece of bacon while Alex poured blueberry syrup that he'd probably whipped up into a large, crystal bowl.

"We slept great, but I thought I'd give Autumn a lie-in. She doesn't get a lot of rest."

"Sleep is vital but don't forget to give the girl some fun too. My David—"

"Wow, Mum. Stop talking." Nate came up behind her and kissed her cheek, giving him and Alex an eye roll.

"I was only saying," Mimi said a little affronted.

"Yeah, well, don't. We all know I was an immaculate conception, and let's leave it at that okay?"

Mimi laughed. "You kids today."

Maggie began to fuss as her hunger took over.

"Is there any baby cereal or something I can feed her? She's just started weaning."

"Yes, we have some Rusk, let me get it."

Mimi showed him the box, and he nodded.

Thirty minutes later, he was wearing more Rusk than Maggie had eaten, but she was happy, and he'd managed to shove a few bites of bacon and pancakes in his mouth.

Jack walked in with Zack and Will and looked at him and Alex before nodding towards the hall. "Can I have a word, please?"

Mitch looked at Mimi who was now chatting with Bebe and Meg. "Can you watch Maggie for just a second?"

"Yes, of course, go on."

Mitch pushed back from the table, and he and Alex followed the others into Zack's office. The room was old and elegant, furnished with a dark walnut desk that was centuries in age, hand-carved bookshelves, and leather couches in dark brown with brass buttons. It screamed old money which it was because Zack was too. Born to the landed gentry, he should've been a politician or a lawyer, but Zack had wanted to serve and had worked hard to make the elite 22 SAS. He was a good man and a great friend, but Mitch's belly dipped at the look in Jack's eye.

"What happened?"

Mitch took a seat on the couch beside Alex, and Will moved to the desk and opened his laptop. Mitch thought it was surgically attached to him, he took it everywhere and he always had a packet of red candy laces on him. Zack was leaning against the bookshelf, his arms crossed, face expressionless as he waited for Jack to begin.

Mitch watched Jack closely as he leaned against the desk, trying to ascertain from his demeanour if the news was bad, but as usual, Jack gave nothing away.

"Lopez found transactions last night that link back to Harold Charles. He's buying up stock of pralidoxime chloride."

Mitch's lips pulled into an angry sneer as he realised what was going on. "That's one of the antidotes for Tabun, right?"

Jack nodded solemnly. "Yeah, the transactions are buried pretty deep within shell companies, but it looks like Harold and Verena haven't fallen out as badly as they would have us believe. We found

114

emails between them suggesting that the family dynamic is far from hostile."

"Are we working on the assumption that they're creating a chemical weapon similar to Tabun and also cashing in on the other end by making the antidote?" Mitch's good mood vanished into thin air as he spoke, the strands unravelling in his head.

"That's my take from it, and the public falling out was a front so we didn't automatically link them."

Alex inclined his head. "How buried are these transactions?"

"Very. It took a lot of digging to find them, but you know Lopez when he gets his teeth into something."

"It's a geek thing," Will said with a shrug.

"We need to get in that warehouse and find out what the fuck is going on." Alex stood and walked to Will. "Pull up the aerial shots of the farm."

Mitch stood and walked over to the desk behind Alex as he pointed at two areas on the screen. "We could go in here and here and do a brute force entry."

"I'd prefer a quick recon. We don't want to tip them off to what we know just yet, or it could accelerate their plans."

Alex and Jack often threw ideas around like this, and neither was worried about disagreeing because the end game was always the same.

Jack looked at Alex and then him. "What are your thoughts, Mitch? You know Linton Allen, what would he do?"

Mitch shook his head. "Hard to say. The kid I knew isn't the man we're hunting. If he's as clever as I think, then he'll be expecting us to find this unless he doesn't know about it. Remember, we don't know how far his and the Cobras' involvement goes. If it were me, I'd bring Hench, Midas, and Anton in, and have Deck question them." Mitch tried to think like Linton, but it was almost impossible. Even the gang he'd so briefly been involved with had evolved into a million-pound operation now.

"We should hit the warehouse at the same time. I agree with Alex on the brute force, but instead of hitting one area hard, hit the Onyx Cobras' base and the warehouse. That way, they won't have time to warn anyone."

"That's a good idea," Jack agreed. "Let's get back to Eidolon and put a plan together."

This was why Mitch had agreed to this job when Jack approached him six years ago. The red tape on the force meant it was a dictatorship. Even though there was no mistaking Jack was the boss at Eidolon, he involved them and listened to them as a team leader should. The salary hadn't hurt either. He was never going to retire comfortably on a police pension, but although the risk was tenfold, so was the pay. He'd never regretted it, not for a second and Jack picking him out of all the excellent armed response and sniper units in the UK was a huge honour.

"Let us know if you need any extra hands." Zack headed for the door. "Until then, I have to help Ava restore order so I don't end up on the sofa."

Will laughed. "Yeah, like that's ever happened."

"First time for everything and she's feeling delicate this morning." Zack lifted his brows and ducked out with a snicker.

"I should get back to Autumn and give her an update before I take her home."

"Meet me at Eidolon in two hours," Jack stated.

"Yeah, sure thing."

Picking up Maggie, who was looking less like she'd fought a battle with her breakfast and lost and more like the angel she was, Mitch took the stairs back to his suite and gently slipped inside.

Autumn was walking out of the bathroom with a towel around her wet body as they came in, her face lighting up at the sight of them. He felt his body harden with desire for her as she scooped Maggie from his arms, and kissed her face, before lifting and hooking an arm around his neck planting her mouth over his for a slow kiss.

"Hmm, now that's what I call a greeting." He held her hips in his hands, knowing she was naked beneath the towel and wanting nothing more than to feel her soft skin against his own.

"I missed you this morning." Her lips twitched with a sultry promise that was hard to ignore.

Lifting his hand, he caressed her cheek. "I thought you might be tired after last night and would appreciate the extra sleep."

"I am, and I did, thank you. I still missed you, though."

Her words made his chest ache in such a way that he wanted to wrap her in his arms and show her his gratitude. "Are you sore?"

Autumn wrinkled her nose as she walked to the bed and set Maggie down. "A little but nothing I can't handle."

"Good, then I can show you how much your words mean to me later tonight."

His lips twitched as she dropped her head before looking at him through her lashes. She was the sexiest woman he'd ever laid eyes on, and she didn't seem to have a clue. Her husband must have been gone in the head to have risked losing a woman like Autumn. Mitch would be eternally grateful that he had though because now he'd show her how she should be treated for the rest of her life if she let him.

He steadied Maggie, who was rolling on the bed with her feet in the air as Autumn grabbed clothes from her overnight bag. It was hard to concentrate when her sexy ass was bent over, but he needed to tell her about Rion and the other developments.

"I have some news."

Autumn straightened her back snapping rigid at the tone he used. She walked to him the pulse beating wildly in her neck and not from desire this time. "Tell me." Her hands gripped his shoulders as she stood between his thighs in only her underwear, and he regretted not waiting until she'd dressed.

Instead of touching her how he wanted, he placed his hands on the outside of her silky thighs. "Hench and Midas, Linton's men visited your family and put a picture of them together on the dark web for us to find."

She didn't freak or become hysterical. "Did they hurt them?" Her words came out on a shaky breath, and he knew it was hard for her despite her composure.

"They're fine. It was a warning." He told her about the rest, and she agreed with the assessment they'd made.

"Will my family be safe once Linton finds out you took his men?"

"We have a man watching Linton and two men watching your family. They aren't Eidolon, but they do some work for us now and again. They're good guys. In fact, they're brothers who served with Jack."

"So they know what they're doing?"

"Yes, Autumn, they're highly skilled men."

Autumn nodded. "Okay."

"Get dressed, honey. Much as I want to sit here and enjoy the view for the rest of the day I have to go into work." Autumn grinned as she spun on her heel and gave him a beautiful view of her butt. "Woman, don't play with me."

"Or what?" she asked in a playful tone which he loved to hear.

He grabbed her around her waist, making her squeal as his hands tickled her ribs. "Or payback will be a bitch." He tickled her again, and she danced around, trying to avoid him before she wrapped her arms around him instead.

"I submit."

"Music to my ears, baby." He kissed her hard and fast before stepping away. "Get yourself dressed."

Mitch dropped Autumn and Maggie off and made sure they were secure in her apartment with everything they needed before he headed in to work. Bebe and Astrid were there, and those two were as dangerous as any man, in fact, more than most men. He knew they'd protect Autumn and Maggie with their dying breath.

It wouldn't come to that, he'd seen his future last night, and it was beautiful. He wouldn't allow either of their pasts to spoil that. It was time to put Linton Allen where he belonged. It made his heart heavy when he thought of the boy he'd known, the younger brother to his best friend who'd looked up to him. He'd always feel some small shard of the blame for what he'd become. Linton could have been anything he wanted with his brilliant mind, but the opportunities weren't the same for kids like them. He'd been lucky, his mum had moved heaven and earth to get him out, but Linton hadn't had that.

He'd taken the wrong path, but to him, it may have seemed like the only path. That he'd made a success of even that showed what he could've become if life and grief hadn't stolen the sweet boy and replaced it with cold evil. Mitch had read the file on Linton as he was now and he couldn't see even a hint of the boy he'd been. Devon would be heartbroken to know what his baby brother had become. He'd joined the Cobras to protect his family, and ultimately it had cost them both. Now Mitch had to face that and put right the wrongs he'd had a part in to save his budding family.

Chapter Nineteen

He would've liked to have seen Autumn before he left, but the window was short, especially as there seemed to be a lot of comings and goings from the Cobras' base. Will had been monitoring the farm with unarmed aerial vehicles commonly known as UAVs from Eidolon while Lopez kept watch on the Cobras.

It was useful for intelligence gathering, but now it was time to act. They'd take the chopper from Hereford at nine o'clock that night and land ten miles north of the farm. Bebe and Astrid would stay with Autumn and Maggie overnight, and Nate would be on call if they needed him. Aubrey was going to pick them up the following morning and drive them into Eidolon where Zack had agreed to meet her and stay with her until they were back.

Mitch had kitted out in the same black clothing as the rest of the team, with his personal body armour underneath, a black helmet with built-in comms, and NVGs. His weapon of choice was his MP5SDs with hollow-point rounds to make sure they didn't over-penetrate and hit a friendly. He also carried a Glock 17 sidearm as well as three K-Bar knives.

"What are the ROE?" Mitch wanted to be fully aware of the rules of engagement on this op as he didn't want blowback.

"Engage on contact, but no kill shots unless fired upon. Alex will run command on the takedown at the Cobras' base, and I'll run point at the farm. Alex, Blake, Reid, and Deck are with you." Jack nodded at Alex. "Mitch, Waggs, Liam, you're with me. Lopez will run comms with Will."

Mitch looked around the helo as they waited to land. Jack had decided that having two bulletproof Range Rovers take them in was preferable than getting too close with the chopper.

"We all good?"

A round of nods happened as the chopper flown by Liam landed in a field owned by the Duchy of Cornwall and sanctioned by the Palace for use on this mission. Mitch was quiet as they got in separate vehicles and headed for the farm and the Cobras' base. He'd asked not to go on that op, worry he'd have to engage someone he knew from his past hanging over him. He would've done it, but

Mitch didn't believe in making life difficult when it wasn't necessary. The fact the Cobras still had the same group of garages on the estate where he'd grown up, despite them dripping in money now, was a statement.

As they approached the farm, Jack killed the lights a mile out and then half a mile later they hid the vehicle in a wooded area before hiking the rest of the way. They were on comms only now and using NVGs to see, the green hue casting an eerie light on the trees and countryside around them.

Jack lifted a fist, and they all stopped, hunkering low on the perimeter of the farm closest to the warehouse which housed the suspected chemical weapons. A group of six vehicles drove in and over twenty-five men walked out of the warehouse and got into the cars before they drove away into the night. That left just four guards on the outside, the heat signatures confirmed by Will.

Mitch waited while Jack checked his watch. The plan was to wait until everyone was in position and hit them all at once. Hench, Anton, and Midas had been confirmed going into the Cobras, if Linton was there it was a bonus. Still, he'd hardly left his mansion which was six clicks east of here in a fucking gated community.

It was impossible with their limited manpower to hit all three locations, and the priority right now was to grab Hench, Midas, and Anton because without his lieutenants Linton would come out in the open where he'd be exposed, and they could grab him as well. That he hadn't left the house in two days was good in that they at least knew where the fucker was.

"On my count." Jack crouched his fist raised. "Go."

They were moving fast, keeping low to the ground as Mitch and Waggs moved off to the left to cover the rear exit. As he stepped into the light, he heard the explosion from the front of the building, set off by Pyro and heard the commotion as the guards went running. As expected, two of them moved to the back door and began firing.

Mitch held back with Waggs four feet to his left returning fire. He could hear as Liam and Jack engaged the guards near the front. A bullet hit close to his right, the wood splintering and bouncing off his helmet before his bullet hit true and the first man went down from a headshot. The plan was they would take some of the men alive and question them.

"One down," he called over the comms.

Waggs hit the second, managing a leg shot as Mitch rushed forward and kicked the gun clear before Waggs bound his hands and legs after a quick check of the wound.

"He'll be fine, it's just a flesh wound."

The sounds of Jack and Liam taking the others out flew over the comms. Happy that the guard was secure, Mitch eased his way inside, lifting his goggles as the harsh lights almost blinded him. The inside the of the space was like a production line, with stations set up containing scales and other drug paraphernalia as they moved towards the front where Liam and Jack were clearing the stacked boxes of any threats. Mitch saw more evidence of cocaine, including a multitude of different distribution methods.

"Look!"

Waggs pointed towards an office space on the second level which was accessed by a mezzanine and gallery area. Most probably an overseer would watch from the there. No cameras had been detected inside, and the lack of guards worried him. Something didn't sit right with this.

Mitch walked up the metal gridded steps and to the office space where he found a locked door.

"Break it open," Jack demanded, and they all stepped back while Liam did the honours.

The lock gave after a few attempts with an axe and what they saw made him shudder. Fridges full of chemicals, centrifuges, syringes, glass burettes, cylinders, not to mention Hydrogen Cyanide, Methylamine, atropine and pralidoxime chloride—it was a fucking nightmare.

"This looks like a loaded weapon." Jack spun, his face frowning. "But it's not enough. This could harm a hundred people, but the volumes they've been buying would be enough to knock out a football stadium."

Liam frowned. "You think we're too late?"

"Or too early." Jack walked to the desk flicking through the papers. "Let's get all this photographed for evidence and get these two assholes back to base for questioning."

Waggs cocked his head. "We gonna leave the drugs?"

"For now. I don't think this is what we're looking for. I think this is a dummy warehouse."

"You mean a second base?" Mitch asked dread settling in his belly like a stone.

"Not sure but this feels wrong." Jack waved his hand in the air. "Let's move. I don't want to be here longer than necessary."

He wasn't sure if it was Jack's words or his actions, but Mitch was on edge as he took pictures of everything in the make-shift lab. Not even hearing that Alex's team had secured Anton, Midas, and Hench made the unease leave his chest.

They walked the two prisoners back through the farmland, the dead bodies of the other two carried between them. A clean-up crew they used would collect them and do what was needed which usually involved a faked accident in these cases.

Eidolon never regretted the lives they took to keep the world safe, but they tried to make sure that it was more comfortable on the families if they could. These men had been nothing but paid pawns, and their families shouldn't suffer for that.

Tipping the dead men into the boot, they secured the other two and headed back towards the helo. They would liaise with a contact from SIS, the secret intelligence service, and then head home. Until then, they had a safehouse they could use twenty miles out from here in the middle of an industrial estate. It was an ex-trap house, disused for years, so Eidolon had bought it and made it secure.

Once the clean-up crew had taken the bodies, Mitch checked his watch, wondering if it was too early to call Autumn. He was surprised to see it was already eight am. He knew she might be on her way to work with Aubrey. It was weird that he missed her so much after only one night apart, but it was the truth. He shot her a quick text to say good morning and tell her he and everyone were safe and well and smiled when his phone rang in his hand, her name on the display.

"Hey."

"Hi, is everyone really okay?"

"Would I lie to you?"

There was a moment of silence at his question. "No, you wouldn't. I trust you, Mitch."

"Good because everyone is fine. We got some of what we needed and should be headed home in the next hour or two. How's my girl?"

Mitch stepped into the living room where Waggs was sleeping sitting up in the chair, his one eye opening as Mitch walked in. Jack and Alex were in the control room with Will and Liam, and Reid was guarding the two men they'd taken who were so far staying silent.

"I assume you mean Maggie."

"Of course. You're my woman, not my girl."

He heard the ownership in his voice and then her sigh, the pleasure in the sound evident. He didn't think he'd ever get tired of the sound of her voice. His hands itched to hold her, to kiss her to just be with her.

"She was a little fussy last night. I think she missed you too."

"I'll be home soon."

"Okay. Aubrey says hello."

"Hi, Aubrey."

"Oh."

Mitch sat straighter at her tone, the knot of apprehension curling in his gut like a snake. "What is it?"

"There's a car stopped in the middle of the road."

He heard Aubrey calling to the driver, and his instincts screamed at him. "Autumn tell Aubrey to get out of there. It's a trap." The room seemed to tunnel so that only her voice mattered as he strained to hear everything.

"Aubrey. Oh my god." Terror rang in her voice before a gunshot echoed in his ear and then a scream penetrated the air, and ice flooded his veins.

Waggs was beside him in a second sensing his fear. "Autumn? Autumn!" he called as the commotion over the line told him his nightmare was coming true.

The silence stretched and then Mitch heard a voice that had aged over the years but still had the familiar undercurrent of intelligence and swagger.

"I guess you're not as clever as you think you are, Mitch." Linton Allen's voice pierced his brain like a knife as his heart beat in his throat.

"Don't you fucking hurt her, or I swear to god I'll rip your fucking heart out with my bare hands." He felt the vein in his head pop as his fist clenched around the phone as if it were Linton's neck

The room was filling his teammates hearing his raised voice. His eyes found Will's and they mirrored how he felt.

"I won't kill her. I need her. But the cop and the brat, well, no promises there."

The click of the line was like an explosion in his ear. Mitch raised his eyes to Will.

"They have them. Linton has Autumn, Aubrey, and Maggie."

Chapter Twenty

The sound of crying wrenched her from the darkness of unconsciousness with a jolt. Autumn fought to sit up as Maggie's cries pierced her brain, the pain in her head making her thoughts feel as if they were wrapped in candy floss. Lifting her hand to her head, she snapped open her eyes when she felt the thick metal cuffs around her wrist and memory flooded back.

Her breathing came fast, an onslaught of emotions hit her with the force of a truck. As her eyes adjusted to the dim light, she realised she was in a small cellar. The walls rough, damp concrete, the bed she was on a fold-away camping cot with a threadbare mattress. Autumn frantically looked around for Maggie, her heart beating wildly, her gut rolling with the bitter acid of bile and terror.

Her baby was nowhere in sight, but she could see a light which she thought was coming from a door at the top of some steps, the source of her baby's cries. Her motherly instinct shot through her as she fell to her knees in her attempt to get to Maggie. Her legs were unbound, and she kept her cuffed hands in front of her as she traversed the darkness, her eyes taking longer than she'd like to adjust.

The effects of whatever Allen had shot into her veins making her movements and reactions slow as she crawled up the steps on hands and knees. Her mind flew from thought to thought, not able to stay focused on her task as snapshots of memory tore into her mind's eye.

Allen stepping up to the car, his gun held steady in front of him. Aubrey's scream as she tried to defend her and Maggie and then the silence as the bullet tore through her friend's abdomen, the blood and shock on her face as she'd looked at Autumn with an apology as if she could have foreseen this. Autumn felt the tears sting the back of her throat as she remembered the horror in Mitch's voice when he'd realised what was going on just a split second before Linton Allen had shot Aubrey.

Finally reaching the top of the wooden steps she felt the breeze of air under the door, saw the light and realised she could no longer hear her baby crying. Anxiety tore through her as she imagined all of the reasons why her child was now silent.

Lifting her hand, her fear for herself gone, she hammered on the door with the flat of her hand.

"Let me out." Her palm slapped loudly, and she heard cursing behind the door and a shadow move closer. "Allen, I swear to god if you hurt her, I'll hunt you down." She screamed until her voice was hoarse and the sound of Maggie crying again had her body sagging in sweet relief.

The lock sliding open on the door had her bracing, moving slightly to the side, so she had the wall for support. Biker booted feet came into view as her gaze travelled up denim-clad legs, a muscular body covered by a white t-shirt then up to the cold, intelligent eyes of Linton Allen.

He cradled Maggie in his arms, who was sucking a dummy that must have been in her bag. Autumn assessed her baby for any signs of injury or pain, her fists clenching with rage that this man dared to touch her. When she found nothing, she blew out the barest of tremulous breaths.

"Stand up." Allen raised his chin, his lip curling in a sneer as he stepped back to give her room. Autumn fought the jagged fury inside her that threatened to rob her of any self-preservation. With her hand pressed to the wall, she lifted from her knees and took a shaky step forward. He didn't hold a gun on her as she stepped into the light, airy kitchen with cream cabinets and black marble work surfaces.

Autumn felt disjointed as she looked around at what was essentially a family home, a large beautiful family home. "Give me my baby." Autumn bit her bottom lip at the way her voice broke, holding her empty arms out for her baby.

"Not yet. First, you need to do something for me."

Allen didn't look like a monster, and yet she'd watched him shoot her husband in cold blood. His features were strong, high cheekbones, mesmerising brown eyes and short-cropped hair. He would've had the world at his feet as intelligent and handsome as he was, but he'd chosen the wrong path.

"What do you want from me?" Her arms fell to her front, the metal of the cuffs rubbing her skin raw. Allen leaned against the counter as Maggie drifted off to sleep in his arms, totally unaware of the danger she faced.

"The formula your husband was working on has a flaw. I need you to fix it."

Autumn shook her head slightly. "I can't just pick up a formula and fix it. That kind of thing takes months of work and I'd need all his research and data analysis."

"You speak like you have a choice, Autumn." The sneer in his voice was mocking and made her take a step forward. His raised eyebrow stopped her short and his mouth quirked into a grin.

"Why are you doing this?"

"Because it's the only way to end this." His voice shook with emotion before he took a breath.

"End what?" Autumn had a feeling in the pit of her belly that she wasn't seeing the entire picture.

"First you agree to help me then I'll tell you."

"Give me Maggie." Autumn knew she was in no position to be making demands, but she had to try at least.

Allen spun, grabbing a gun from the counter behind him and she froze, sickness forcing its way up her throat, but then he threw her a key. "Uncuff yourself."

Autumn did as he asked, making slow movements before dropping the metal shackles to the ground. Allen moved quickly, making her jump, but instead of a blow, she felt the weight of her baby in her arms. Never had it felt so good as she hugged her tightly to her body, taking in the clean scent of her child, the ache in her chest easing.

"She's been fed and changed." Autumn looked at the man before her with utter confusion. "I don't understand."

Allen hitched up on to the barstool at the breakfast bar. "I'm everything they say I am, Autumn. I'm a killer, I torture people and hurt them, but I didn't kill your husband, and I'd never hurt a child, not ever," he enunciated with venom.

"I saw you kill Terrell."

"No, you saw Anton kill Terrell, except he made it look like it was me." He shook his head slowly. "Think about it, Autumn. Who was the first person to arrive at your house after Terrell was killed?"

Autumn thought back to that night, suddenly questioning what she'd seen. It had been dark as Terrell shoved her into the closet. She remembered Allen slamming the door open, seeing him in profile, the tattoo on his hand clearly visible, his hair and height an exact match.

"But I saw your tattoo. It was you."

"Who pointed out the tattoo as being mine?"

Anton, he'd been the one to find her, to ask if the shooter had a tattoo or any distinguishing marks.

Autumn looked up as the sudden realisation hit. "But why?"

"Terrell got cold feet, wanted out, but Anton needed him to finish the formula. Then he hit on the idea to involve you instead."

"But why frame you? You run the Onyx Cobras. He's nothing but a soldier."

"I run the Cobras, but I wanted no part of this. The people I hurt and kill know what they're involved with. Innocent people living clean lives being hit by chemical weapons? I'd never get involved with that."

"And yet you are involved, you're up to your neck in it." Autumn began to pace, her fear for this man waning as she began to see the man behind the mask.

"Anton, Hench, and Midas got us involved. I had to go along, or I'd lose my position as leader of the Cobras. The only way I can control the narrative is by being in charge. My reputation isn't something I've nurtured because I'm an egotist, it's so people fear crossing me."

"So why did Anton, Hench, and Midas do it? Why did they go behind your back and why frame you for murder?"

"Because I've been trying to take the club clean, which means less of a cut for them. Anton doesn't know I know about him killing Terrell. He believes I'm a fool who's losing his grip and hell, maybe I am." He brushed a hand over his face in a gesture of exhaustion.

"You let them think you're losing control to give them enough rope to hang themselves with."

"Yes." He looked at her consideringly. "But we have an even bigger problem than my handle on the club. Anton is bringing in someone else to finish the formula. I told him I wanted you so that you'd pay for Terrell's crimes. He liked the perverse notion, so here we are."

"You shot Aubrey."

"No, I shot Aubrey with a blank. It will cause a flesh wound at most. I had to make it seem real. I need Mitch to believe so he'll come for me. You need to give him enough time to figure this out and end this once and for all by stopping that formula from working."

"You want me to stop the formula from working?"

"Yes, the people at Henderson are close, but I told them I want you to finish it. I need you to make it look like you're fixing it but don't. We can't allow this to go out into the open and kill people."

"Why now? Why, after everything you've done have you developed a conscience?"

Allen shrugged. "I lost my way. I joined the Cobras because I knew taking them over was the only way to destroy them. They took my brother, my best friend, and I killed every last one of them for it when I gained power, but then I lost my way. Began to believe my own press, got high on the power, the women, the drugs."

"What made you see the light?"

"I'm not sure I have, but even I have my limit, and dealing in chemical weapons is it."

"If I do this, how do I know you'll let me go?"

"I won't have to because Mitch and his friends will find you. They already have Anton, Hench, and Midas. They'll throw me under the bus to save themselves, and he'll come."

"He'll kill you." Autumn felt sadness well in her chest for this broken man who had been a grief-stricken boy.

"I know."

"You want to die?"

"I'm tired of it all. So many deaths, so much blood on my hands, I'm unredeemable."

"Nobody is unredeemable." Yet as she said the words, she knew that wasn't true. Some people were, but she didn't think Allen was one of them.

"Don't feel sorry for me, Autumn. I'm not worth any one's sorrow."

"You could confess and help them take everyone down?"

"Do you know what would happen to me in prison? A nark, a snitch? I'd be dead anyway. At least this way I go out by my own choice."

Tears bristled in her eyes as she saw that the man she'd been running from was more tortured than she'd ever been. "Fine, I'll help you, but you must do something for me first."

Allen smirked. "You're not in a position to make deals, Autumn."

"Yes, I am, and we both know it, or I wouldn't be here. I want you to make a note of everything you have on Anton. That man is evil and he needs to be locked up. I don't want him to get off on a technicality."

"Fine. Now we need to go."

"What about Maggie? I don't want Harold Charles or Verena Finch anywhere near my daughter."

"They won't be. They never come anywhere near the business end."

"I still don't want her near this. It's a fucking chemical weapon. A lab is no place for a baby."

"Better make sure you're careful then because the only way this happens is if she goes too." He bent closer. "Verena wanted her as leverage."

"That bitch."

Allen chuckled. "I see why Mitch loves you. You're all right, Autumn Roberts."

Autumn said nothing; her brain was still trying to grasp the revelations of the last twenty minutes and wondering how this would be affecting Mitch.

Chapter Twenty-One

Mitch had never felt so afraid in his entire life, despair pitted in his belly, making him feel faint. Beside him, Will sat silently, his usually relaxed good humour vanished as Liam flew them, Jack, and Waggs home.

Home—a place he'd used to sleep until he'd met Autumn, then it had quickly become a place he treasured, a sanctuary he craved. Now Linton—no, from now on he was *Allen*, the boy he'd known as Linton no longer existed—had her and Maggie. His fist clenched against his thigh as he imagined what might be happening and hoped his imagination was worse than the truth.

When Aubrey had been shot, Will had lost it. Only Jack had been able to get through to him long enough to calm him down. The bond between the brothers was evident for every man to see as Jack, who was shaken himself took control, calling Fortis and having Zack and Daniel at the scene in minutes had eased Will's frayed grasp on reality.

As they landed at the back of Eidolon, Mitch and Will were out of the chopper in seconds, running for the car park.

"I'll drive." Jack was opening the locks on the Range Rover as they jumped in and he floored it towards Fortis.

Zack had taken Aubrey there to be assessed by their private doctor once Daniel had triaged her injuries and determined that it was a flesh wound. Will had barely been mollified, threatening every man and his dog with death and pain.

When they got to Fortis fifteen minutes later, Will raced towards the medical room as Mitch walked behind him at a slower pace. He was concerned for Aubrey, but his worry for Autumn and Maggie overshadowed everything.

"How is she?" he asked as Nate moved down the hallway.

Nate stopped with his hands on his hips. "She'll be fine. It was just a scratch. The shooter used a blank. We found the casing at that scene. Figured you'd want it cleaned up before the cops got there."

"Thanks, Nate, appreciate it."

"Anytime, I just hate that you're going through this, worst fucking feeling in the world."

"Yeah, you went through something similar with Skye."

"Yep, I still have nightmares about it." Nate slapped him on the shoulder. "We'll get them back."

Mitch nodded as Jack came out of the medical room and closed the door behind him.

"She really okay?"

"Yeah, she will be. My brother, not so much. I think he just lost ten years of his life."

"I know how he feels."

"We need to get back to Eidolon and find out what happened. I called Xander, who was watching the house, and he assures me Allen never left the property."

Xander and his brothers ran a troubleshooting company. They went into a company and turned it around, oftentimes, buying it up. Xander Lawson had been in the SAS with Jack, his brothers in different branches of the military. They had done a few jobs for them before, but this was a favour.

"You sure you trust him?" Mitch had never doubted Xander or any of the Lawson brothers, but right now, his trust issues were at an all-time high.

"Yeah, he'd never turn, that man would cut off his own arm before he saw a woman or child hurt. He has a teenage daughter so he feels pretty strongly about this."

Mitch nodded as he and Jack headed back to Eidolon, where he knew Liam would have already started working this case. He walked in and found maps spread out on the conference room desk.

"I think I know how he got out," Liam said in greeting

Mitch moved swiftly to see the maps of Allen's home. It was nothing like the home he'd grown up in and screamed affluence and middle-class. "How?"

"See this?" Liam pointed at a small section at the edge of the property.

Mitch leaned in close to get a better look. "What is it?"

"An underground decommissioned missile silo. It was sold off in the 1980s when the cold war ended. Allen's property borders it here. Want to guess where it ends?"

"The Farm," Mitch said excitement tinging his tone and adrenalin surged.

"Bingo. I spoke to Lopez, and he has Allen coming out of the A4179, close to the farm last night."

"So, as we were arriving, he was leaving to kidnap Autumn and Maggie." Fury stole through his tone, making his voice sound like broken glass.

"Yes, CCTV puts him driving up to the farm about two hours after we left. He drove into that barn of the far east corner."

"I bet that's where the chemical weapons are produced. A silo gives them everything they need, including privacy and silence. They can go unnoticed by everyone."

"That's why we only found a fraction of what we expected at the farm," Mitch surmised.

"I need to call Reid and Deck. I want him to concentrate on pulling all the information they can from Anton, Hench, Midas."

"I'll load the chopper with everything we need. We can put a plan together and get your girls back."

Liam slapped him on the shoulder as he walked out. Mitch knew it wasn't as simple as that. They knew where they were, but they had to get them out without anyone getting hurt. He walked towards Autumn's office, pushing open the door and stepping inside. Her scent hit him instantly, the sweet honeysuckle smell wrapping around him like fragrant summer rain.

He strolled to her desk chair, his fingers trailing over the cot where the little angel that had stolen his heart took her naps. He'd never considered kids all that much, yet now he couldn't imagine his life without her in it. Her belly laughs, the way her face lit up when she saw him, made him warm from the inside out. He wanted more of that, more time with Maggie but also more children that shared Autumn's beauty and brains. He wanted a future with the woman he loved and had been too afraid to express it to.

It seemed like such a silly thing to hold back, the expression of love for another. The truth was he'd been scared of being vulnerable, of opening his heart and having it rejected. Now though, he'd shout it from the rooftops, tell the world he loved her if he was only given a chance. He didn't care if she said it back, because she showed it with every single action, with her trust. The way she put her faith in him to keep her and Maggie safe, and he'd failed her.

Sitting heavily, he took out his phone, pulling up the pictures he'd taken of him and Autumn the night of the party. Autumn was grinning widely into the camera with that sexy grin he loved so much as she leaned into his body. Had it really only been less than forty-eight hours since he'd made love to her? Felt her body tighten around him with desire, seen the pleasure flash across her face.

His world had toppled on its head in that time, and he fought the agony her absence brought, wetness tingling behind his eyes at the helpless sensation he felt, knowing she was scared, that she could be hurt and he was impotent until they had a plan.

His instinct wanted him to get in his car and drive to Allen's house and demand he release them, but he knew an action like that would be foolish. Even now, with his world in danger, he was the sensible one, but calm had escaped him.

He fought the emotion, knowing if he gave in to it, he'd crumble beneath the weight of it. He prayed for the first time in more years than he could remember to a god he wasn't even sure he believed in anymore that they were safe. That Linton Allen would find the last shred humanity in his heart and spare them from pain or death.

Scrolling through his contacts, he dialled the one woman who could bring him peace while his heart was in danger.

"Hey, Ma."

"Mitch, how lovely to hear your voice. I was just thinking about you. How is that precious girl of yours?"

His throat clogged, and a sob burst through his closed fist. "Not so good, Ma."

"Mitchell? Talk to me, tell me what's wrong?"

Swallowing, he cleared his throat with a cough. "Nothing, Mum, it's all good."

"Don't lie to me. I'm your mother and I can hear the pain in your voice as clear as day."

"You remember I said we were helping Autumn with some issues in her past?"

"Yes."

"They caught up to her, Mum. I failed her."

"Is she alive?" He heard the trace of fear in his mother's voice as her accent deepened.

"I fucking hope so. I don't know what I'll do if she isn't."

"She's alive and you, my boy, are going to get her back. I know you, you have the heart of a lion, and if you love her, you'll fight for her."

"I do love her, Mum, so much and I haven't even told her yet."

"There will be time for that later, I feel it. She'll be okay. A woman worthy of my son will fight."

"There's more. Linton Allen is the man who took her." Mitch kept talking, explaining everything to the woman who'd sacrificed so much for him. As he spoke, he felt calmer; renewed energy flooded his veins.

"I always felt bad for leaving that boy with his no-good family. He came to visit me, you know. Years later, when you were in the police force as an officer. He said he was happy you got out, but that his path was different to yours and the only way he could avenge Devon was by breaking it from the inside out. I never understood what he meant, but I always felt sad for that boy. He could have been so much more if he'd only had a chance."

Mitch sat straighter in the chair. "How come you never told me?"

"I didn't want the past to influence the present."

"I'm going to kill him if he hurts them. I don't care about the cost, he *will* pay."

"I wish I could take this pain from you, Mitch, but you've always been your own man. I know the job you do is dangerous, and I know you hide it from me or try to, but know this, I trust you to do what is right."

"Thanks, Mum. That means a lot. I love you."

"I love you too, my boy, so much."

Mitch hung up, his mother's revelations ringing in his ears. She believed in him wholeheartedly, and he knew Autumn did too. It was time he believed in himself and went and got his girls back.

Standing, he pushed the chair in and closed the office door. It was time to go to war for the woman he loved. He just prayed the only casualties were the ones on the wrong side.

Chapter Twenty-Two

Autumn glanced at the man holding some sort of semi-automatic weapon on the outside door of the small make-shift lab. Her nerves frayed with every second she spent in this room with her baby not six feet from the dangerous chemicals.

When she'd set foot inside the silo earlier that morning, she'd been unable to hide her awe at the scale on which the operation ran. What's more, it was entirely under the radar of the authorities.

It was a vast warren of tunnels with labs, storage, even a small kitchen and bathroom with bunks to the left of it. Full electricity ran through it—powering the fridges, along with equipment she knew cost thousands of pounds.

It also told of the brilliance of the man who stood with his arms crossed at the far end of the lab where she worked. Allen was a bad person, he may not have done the things she'd thought he had, but he'd done some nasty shit. Murder, assault, kidnap, extortion, and drug dealing to name the ones she knew of, but she couldn't help feeling some small bit of empathy for him.

Linton Allen had set this up with nobody knowing. She could only imagine what he could've achieved with the right support. He'd also been considerate of her needs since he'd kidnapped her, which was in no way a compliment, but he could've been cruel, and he wasn't.

He'd set up a cot for Maggie in a bedroom where he'd made sure she had food and water. The door was locked, but it was clean and dry, and Maggie had been none the wiser thank god.

A phone rang, and she turned to look at Allen. He frowned as he walked to where she was pretending to mix chemicals.

"We need twenty-four hours." He hung up and his face was harsh with anxiety. "Mitch needs to move. Verena is putting pressure on to find the formula or she'll outsource it. She has a biochemical weapons expert flying in tomorrow, and if you haven't done as she's asked, they'll kill you." He glanced at Maggie, his jaw flexing. "And her."

"No, you have to do something."

"I can't fucking do anything. Mitch needs to come through."

"Just call him. They can help us."

"No, I told you that's not how this goes down."

His tone was final, and she knew he wouldn't relent. This was the play he was making for better or worse, and she just had to pray Eidolon was as good as she believed. She had to try another tactic. "What did you want to be when you were a kid, Linton?"

Allen glared as he crossed his arms again. His body turned so that his back was partial to the door. "I don't remember."

"Oh, come on, indulge me. You're putting the life of my baby in danger for your pride. It's the least you can do."

"I don't owe you anything, lady."

"No, maybe not." She shrugged as she brought up the analysis on the screen in front of her. "But you were the one who brought me here, brought my sweet innocent child into this mess. You could have left Maggie behind. Could've just taken me but you didn't, you took her too. If something happens to her, Mitch will kill you."

Allen stared at Maggie. "She was a means to an end. Not a person but a bargaining chip I could use to control you."

"How can you look at life in that way?"

"Because anything else will make you weak, will make you vulnerable, and I can't afford that weakness."

"Love isn't a weakness. It's strength."

"Not for everyone."

"You never been in love?" She was running out of options now of trying to get him to see a different way out.

Allen was silent, and Autumn sighed in defeat, perhaps there was no getting through to him, maybe the human part of this was gone.

It was seven hours later as they walked back down the tunnel that linked his home to this underground weapons plant that he answered her.

"I wanted to be a doctor, a kid's doctor."

Autumn cocked her head as Maggie snuggled against her shoulder. "Yeah, I think you'd have been good at that."

Allen chuckled humourlessly. "Nah, kids are scared of me."

"Maggie isn't," she stated. "She fell asleep in your arms yesterday."

"Yeah well, the kid obviously has about as much self-preservation as her mother."

"No, kids are like animals, they can sense things. Maggie knows you won't hurt her."

His face hardened. "Don't push your luck, Autumn. You won't change my mind, and emotional blackmail won't work on me."

Autumn said no more; she had a feeling it was in the lap of the gods now. She just wished there was a way to contact Mitch. She knew he'd be going out of his mind with worry. The last kiss they'd shared came into her mind later that night as she lay in bed. It had been sweet and sensual and full of all the things she wished she'd said to him.

Mitch Quinn had changed her life, shown her what a true partnership looked like and she'd fallen in love with him. It hadn't been her choice to fall in love, but rather a beautiful shock from the blue, and it was something she'd cherish no matter what happened in the next few days.

Her only wish was that Maggie stayed safe, that her baby lived a long, healthy life. It wasn't giving up, she'd fight with everything she had, but the rest was up to the fates and the men of Eidolon.

Knocking on the door, she waited for Allen to open it.

"What do you want?"

He'd said little to her since the conversation in the tunnel, and she was okay with that, what more was there left to say?

"Can I have a piece of paper and a pen, please?"

"Why?"

"I want to leave a note for Mitch in case I don't make it out of this alive."

Allen watched her for a long moment, his face a mask she couldn't read. Then he closed the door in her face. Sighing, Autumn sat on the bed, her back going straight when he opened the door again and shoved a pen and notepad at her.

"Thank you." She smiled at him with hesitance.

Allen nodded and stepped back, closing the door with finality.

Autumn began to write, not knowing how to start such a letter but knowing she had to at least try and express in words how she felt. It was one of the things that had hurt most when Terrell died, not being able to express her feelings.

The following morning when the door to her jail opened, she handed Allen the letter.

"If this goes wrong, make sure Mitch gets this letter please."

138

He eyed it before nodding and placing it on his kitchen table.

Today was the day, she felt it in her bones. By the time the sun went down this would be over, she just prayed her smiley Roo would be safe.

* * *

"What's he saying?" Mitch nodded to Anton, who was sat in the middle of the room with a bag over his head.

Decker grinned, and it was the coldest thing Mitch had ever seen. "Oh, he's very talkative, wants the world to know how clever he is, how great and totally contradicting the other two."

"What about the other two?"

"They gave Allen up in a heartbeat. Told us how he killed Terrell, how he set up the deal with Henderson, where the silo entrance is on his property."

"Nice." Mitch crossed his arms, a sneer curling his lips. He might hate Allen but that these men would give him up so easily made him uneasy.

"Oh yeah, they're real treasures," Deck said with a mocking grin that didn't reach his eyes.

"What's Anton saying?" Mitch and Deck kept their voices low, so the man who was tied up didn't hear.

"He reckons he killed Terrell, that he masterminded the deal with Henderson. He says Allen has lost his nerve, that he didn't want to get involved."

"What do you think?" Mitch valued Decker's opinion; he was the smartest mind he knew and could read people better than anyone.

"I believe Anton is telling the truth. I'm not saying he's the sharpest tool in the box, but he is behind the deal and the murder of Autumn's husband."

Mitch clenched his fist at the reference to Terrell. "If that's the case, none of this makes sense. Why would Allen leave Anton alive knowing he went behind his back, and who is really running the Cobras?"

"Allen is most definitely in charge still, but I get the feeling there's dissent within the gang."

"I want to talk to him."

Deck nodded as he and Mitch stepped towards Anton. Waggs, Reid, and Blake were with Hench, and Alex and Jack were questioning Midas.

Dragging the hood from his head with a jerk, Mitch glared at Anton Williams. "I hear you're the mastermind behind this chemical weapons deal."

Anton's greedy eyes lit up with pride. "Yes, I am."

"Seems we have ourselves a player." He glanced at Deck with chuckle and Anton gave a nervous laugh.

"Allen thinks he's in charge, but he'll soon see who's really calling the shots at the Cobras."

"Not Allen then?"

"No, he's lost it. He wouldn't take the deal, didn't want us involved with chemical weapons. Thinks that innocent lives will be lost, but I showed him."

Mitch could see the excitement in his eyes. "Yeah, how so?"

"Verena knows he's weak. If she doesn't hear from me in the next twelve hours she'll have her team kill every man in the silo, including Allen."

Mitch's gut tightened at the truth he heard in the man's words. "Why kill Terrell though if he was the mind behind the formula?"

"Terrell handed his balls to his wife. She wanted him out, so he tried to bail. Allen was going to let him, but I showed that idiot. I killed him and made it look like Allen. I was so close to getting rid of Allen."

Mitch rubbed his bottom lip before leaning back on his heels and crossing his arms. "So, let me get this straight. You killed your brother-in-law, set Allen up for the fall, brokered the deal for the chemicals, and have a failsafe in case you get caught?"

"Exactly."

"But you'll still end up in jail for all that."

Anton laughed. "I'll run the Cobras from the inside, don't be a fool, man. I have the power now. Allen will die and will make my men rich."

"Hench and Midas in on this?"

"Yes, they hated the direction Allen was taking the Cobras too. He suddenly grew a conscience like a fucking pussy."

"Who checks the silo operation?"

"Allen does daily but not for long. Verena will kill him soon, wipe out his entire team and put ours in."

"How many men?"

"Allen has twenty soldiers, but Verena is sending in double that amount."

Mitch tipped his head. "Are you really that stupid, Anton, or is this a game?"

"What the fuck does that mean?" Anton's arrogance had turned to bluster now.

"Well, if Verena has the silo set up, has the people to work on the formula, what does she need you for?"

"I'm her right-hand man."

"You're a fucking moron. You're as good as dead, you just don't know it."

"No, you need to help me." The panic made his voice rise two octaves.

"If I had my way, I'd personally deliver you to her with a fucking bow on for what you've put Autumn through."

"No come on, man. I protected her. I kept her safe."

Mitch's fist slammed into Anton's jaw as his calm composure snapped. Bending close to the whimpering man he kept his voice low. "You fucking liar, you almost ruined her, and I'm going to enjoy watching you squirm when they find out what a little snitch you are."

Mitch walked from the room as Decker gagged his mouth and covered his head again. He needed a minute to get his head around things. Pushing outside, he felt the fresh night air on his skin, the smells of the countryside familiar to him now. He'd spent the last few weeks hating Allen for what he'd done to Autumn, but he was innocent of that, he was also not guilty of killing her husband. Guilt for thinking the worst of the boy he'd known hit his chest, and he put a hand against the wall of the building to catch his breath.

Deck stepped out lighting a rare cigarette, the glow bright in the darkness of the night. "You okay?"

"Yeah, just trying to sort it in my head."

"Seems simple to me."

141

Mitch lifted his head, cocking it to the side. "Yeah?"

"Allen is destroying the Cobras from the inside. He knew you'd come for Autumn and wants us to take down the lab."

"With Anton and the others in custody, the gang will fall apart, lose power and implode from the inside." Mitch began to pace his mind whirling with possibilities, and then what his mother said struck him. "He planned this all along."

Deck frowned. "What?"

"I was talking to my mum earlier, and she said Allen visited her years ago before he joined the Cobras. He told her he was on a different path to me and the only way to avenge his brother was from the inside out." Mitch looked at Decker with shock. "He planned this all along, to take control and then destroy the gang that took his brother."

"We need to talk to the others, because if we don't make our play before dawn, then Verena Finch will send in her team to slaughter them all."

And Autumn and Maggie would be in the line of fire with him.

Chapter Twenty-Three

Mitch crouched low to the ground, his mind focused on the job ahead, as the stillness of the night cloaked him and the team. He'd wanted to go straight to Allen, walk into the lion's den and face the man who'd taken his woman and child but there hadn't been time. Lopez had picked up chatter that a hit was gonna go down an hour before dawn at the silo.

Eidolon needed to be in position to mitigate the threat before Autumn and Maggie could be hurt. The guards inside the silo would either come quietly or die. Jack always believed that they couldn't seek retribution if they were dead, although he tried to keep the enemy alive if they had a use to him.

"This is Q in position."

"Pyro check."

"King check."

The different team members began to check in with Jack holding the last line. "Boss man, check."

As the explosion rent the air, he was already moving, his night vision device allowing him to see as the rats began to scurry from the den. He fired shot after shot as men came at him with guns, dropping them where they stood, their faces a mask of shock. He kept moving through the warren of tunnels until he came upon the lab.

Stepping through he cleared the room, knowing Waggs had his back as he listened over the earpiece as the team efficiently took down the threat to humanity at worst and at best, several hundred people.

Stopping next to the cot, he could smell the scent of the woman he loved over the gunpowder and chemicals. It called to him like a siren's song, teasing his senses that she was close or had been. Looking around, he couldn't see her anywhere.

"They aren't here." His face was a savage mask, the line of his lips harsh with fear and retribution. Allen may not be what he'd thought, but he'd still brought her into this danger.

"Boss man, Doc, and Q are moving to stage two. Let's go."

Mitch led the way from the lab and followed the tunnel that led to the house that Allen owned. The dark walls lit by crude lights, as he got closer he lifted his NVGs and then stopped, his hand lifting to stop Waggs' forward momentum.

Mitch cocked his ear, listening to the sound again, his eyes on Waggs and he knew when he heard it too.

Gunshots!

He was running before he realised what was happening, his feet moving him closer with a desperation he'd never known before. Stopping at the exit, he took a moment to look around and saw four vehicles surrounding Allen's Linton's house.

"Boss man, this is Q, we have four tango's vehicles at the house."

"Do not engage. We're coming to you."

"Negative, shots fired inside."

Mitch heard Jack curse, but he didn't respond, he knew Mitch would be careful, he also knew he wasn't going to wait when the women he loved was in there and in danger. He looked at Waggs who nodded; he knew his friend would follow him into hell if he had to.

Running across the open grass, he skirted the edges so the motion detector wouldn't pick up their approach. The back door was partially open, and he heard a voice coming from the living room. Blood covered the kitchen floor as they entered silently, and Mitch had to fight the enraged panic blooming inside him. He had to believe they were safe, or he wouldn't be able to do this.

His heart beat wildly and his hand was far steadier on the weapon he used than he'd have thought. Only training and sheer will keeping him from losing his mind right then. He'd kill every man that had touched her or Maggie. Their safety was his only concern. He loved her with so much passion he knew without a doubt he wouldn't survive losing her.

Through the glass double doors that led into the living room, he saw Verena Finch talking to two men, her face an arrogant mixture of evil and confidence. Her blue pinstripe suit didn't befit the occasion yet somehow telling the story of her superiority or at least how she saw herself.

"We're in position, and the tangos outside are down."

Knowing they could move but still not seeing Allen, Maggie, or Autumn, Mitch looked at Waggs who nodded at the sofa blocking their view of the floor at Verena's feet. Hope bloomed in his chest when he heard Autumn's voice, clear and robust.

"You won't get away with this, you sick bitch."

Never had a sound been so beautiful to him. He didn't allow himself the moment of relief because the danger was still imminent.

"Verena, you can do whatever you want with me but let them go."

Allen, but the timbre of his voice held barely concealed pain, the rasp of his breathing told Mitch he was badly injured.

"I have no use for you. You were nothing but a pawn. Now the base is set up, it's time for you to die with her."

Mitch eyed the two men who wore black masks over their faces and were armed with MP5s through the scope of his rifle. His finger squeezed the trigger, and the first man fell seconds before the other man went down too. The shots were clean and deadly and the shock on Verena's face morphed into fear before she turned to run, only to barrel into Alex and Reid.

Her screams of indignation and fury sounded in the night, but his only thought was Autumn and Maggie. He ran towards her, the raw expression of relief and love filling her face almost unmanning him. He slid to his knees and opened his arms, grasping her and Maggie, who was in her arms, to his chest in a crushing hold close to his heart. Mitch buried his head in her hair, inhaling her sweet scent, glad he was on his knees as he would've fallen to them as the emotion hit him.

He ran his hands over her body, checking for injury before he pulled back and looked into her eyes full of tears. "Are you both okay?"

Autumn nodded. "Yes, Linton saved us."

Mitch looked down then, noticing for the first time Allen was on the floor beside her covered in blood from a shot to the chest. He was barely conscious, his eyes on Mitch and Autumn, a small smile playing at his lips which resembled the boy he'd been.

Mitch wanted to feel hate, to let the anger inside him boil over for what he'd done but found nothing, just relief that he had the woman he loved and her sweet baby, who was now splitting the air with her cries, in his arms again.

"Mitch, help him. Please."

Her desperate sob had him frowning as he looked to her and then to the man he'd known, whose lifeblood was soaking into the cream rug beneath his body. He'd caused so much hurt, so much pain, and Mitch needed that to end.

Releasing her, he held his hand over Allen's wound, a groan of pain slipping past his lips as Mitch applied pressure.

"Doc," he called, suddenly wanting Linton Allen to live.

Waggs was beside him in a second his hands working fast, cutting open the cloth of Linton's shirt and using Quickclot to stem the bleed. Mitch removed his hands covered in blood and felt only regret that it had ended this way.

"Always knew you would be the one to end this." Allen's voice was weak.

"No, you did that. You set out to destroy the Cobras, and it worked."

Allen closed his eyes in peace at last, and Mitch grasped his hand. "No dying."

Allen's eyes sprang open, but they were glassy now. "I'm sorry."

"So am I, Linton," he said, seeing the boy he'd once been in that moment. "I should've stayed or looked out for you when Devon died, and I didn't. I was a coward."

Mitch felt emotion clog his throat as he remembered the good times he'd had as a child on his poor London estate home. They'd played, rode bikes, and been brothers, Devon and Linton almost living at his home. It was only as they grew that things changed, that he and Devon got dragged into a world that was virtually impossible to escape.

"No, you tried to save him, I know you did. I never blamed you, Mitch. I'm happy you found a beautiful life." Allen glanced behind him, and Mitch turned to see Autumn cuddling Maggie, tears flowing freely down her cheeks.

Mitch glanced back his old friend. "I want you to know that."

"Too late for me."

"Don't say that, you'll live or I'll kick your ass."

"Time to move," Waggs said as a stretcher appeared beside him between Alex and Blake.

Waggs and Mitch lifted Allen onto the stretcher and carried him to the private ambulance that was waiting outside. Allen was loaded in, and the two doctors on the Eidolon payroll took over. Mitch stepped back, his hands falling to his sides before Autumn slipped under his arm, and he held her tight, watching as the ambulance drove away. It was doubtful Allen would make it, and even if he did, he faced years in prison for the crimes he'd committed.

Turning his back on the pain he knew would come later, he faced Autumn. "Are you sure you're both all right?"

"Yes, he treated us okay. He has so much regret it's hard not to feel for him. How is Aubrey?"

"Fine, just a flesh wound, although Will wants Allen's heart on a spit for it."

"The others?" she asked as they walked towards the house where Jack was organising the clean-up like the chief he was.

"Anton killed Terrell. He set up the chemical weapons deal, and Hench and Midas were in on it. They didn't like what they saw as Allen's weakness or the fact it would hurt their profits."

"Money and power." Her voice held sadness but not shock at his words.

He took Maggie from her arms, kissing her and taking the baby softness of her body as she settled into his hold with trust. His other arm around Autumn, he pulled her close. "I thought I'd lost you. Thought I'd missed my chance to tell you how much I love you." Autumn went still as they stopped walking a little way out from the noise of the now active crime scene. He looked at her as her bottom lip wobbled and a tear slid down her face. "I never thought I could love like this, but I do. I love you so damn much I can hardly breathe sometimes."

Her hand rested on his chest, her touch steadying him, even as he felt the slow burn of need seep through his skin at her touch. "I love you too, Mitch. You came into my life like a hurricane, and swept away all my doubts, took away all my problems, and left me with a feeling of being cherished and adored. You gave me back something that the man who should've loved me and Maggie took away. You gave me back my worth."

"Oh, sweetheart, you're priceless to me. Nothing in this world is more important to me than you, Maggie, and any other children we might have."

Her perfectly arched brows rose in surprise. "You want children with me?"

Mitch bent to catch her mouth in a slow chaste kiss that was somehow more intimate than anything he'd felt with anyone else. "Honey, I want lots of babies with you. I want to fill a football stadium with little Autumns."

"I want that too, although not a football stadium."

He kissed her again then, and something that had broken inside him when his friend died healed. It was over, and the only way forward held beauty beyond his ability to comprehend.

* * *

Jack stood over the bed of the man who had shot his sister-in-law, a woman he loved like a sister, was family to him, and held out the piece of paper. "If you accept this your old life is gone, you'll be dead, and anyone you know will believe that to be the case. Your money, your contacts, family, friends all gone, but you'll be free."

Allen looked back at him, his cold stare full of intelligence and regret, the weight of his actions so heavy on his soul that Jack wasn't sure he'd ever be whole again. "What do you get out of this?"

Jack respected the question. This man was barely alive, only the quick thinking of the surgeons had saved him, and yet he still questioned the hand that offered him a way out. That was just the kind of careful, suspicious, dangerous man he needed inside the network he was building.

Jack had realised in the last year that having good men inside Eidolon wasn't enough. He needed people inside the underbelly of the criminal world—men and women who could blend in as Bás did.

Rykov Anatolievich had been the first person he'd approached for this mutually beneficial alliance. When they'd first met five years ago, he'd been rising through the ranks of the Russian Bratva, now he was the man giving the orders. Rykov was cruel, deadly, and swift to punish anyone who even questioned his word. But he was also smart, and he knew having Eidolon as an enemy would cost him more than a tentative peace treaty would.

Eidolon would stay out of his way as long as Jack never had cause to doubt his promise to stay away from the UK with his illegal business dealings and Rykov would pass them information when needed. Now Jack had forged similar relationships with other networks around the globe.

"I get eyes and ears in places only the lost live."

"If I refuse?"

"Then you'll go to a maximum-security prison for the rest of your life for the crimes you've committed." Jack was a matter of fact, but he wanted this.

Allen would be an excellent asset to have despite his wrongdoings and the blood that soaked his hands. That Will had suggested it, despite the fact that this man had hurt Aubrey, showed the importance of this deal, but Jack wouldn't show his hand.

"Not much of a choice really."

Jack shrugged. "Not my concern."

"What about Mitch? Will he know?"

"My men are not pawns. They're the lifeblood of Eidolon and secrets have a way of poisoning that, so yes he'll know, they all will."

"I want Mitch as my contact inside Eidolon."

"No." Jack knew his play was to manipulate, and he'd never put Mitch in danger like that. "I won't have Mitch compromised."

"Then who?"

"Whoever I see fit." Jack wouldn't allow him to call the shots on this. He was either in or out. He handed Allen a card with just a handwritten number on it, turned, and headed for the door. "The offer expires at midnight."

Jack drove the short way back to the office to wait for his answer.

At five minutes to midnight, the call came to confirm Linton Allen was dead and a new asset now worked for Eidolon.

Epilogue

Autumn watched her husband as he carried their daughter on his strong shoulders. The sound of her giggles, the way he protected her and showered with so much love, melted her heart every single time she saw it, which was often.

Mitch was an amazing father to Maggie, as she knew he'd be to the child that grew in her belly. She'd never regret the day she met him and second to giving birth to Maggie, her wedding six months ago had been the happiest day of her life.

With just their families and friends, it had been a celebration of the love they shared, choosing the place where she'd first realised she loved him for the wedding. Ava and Zack had graciously offered the Estate and Mimi and Helen had done the flowers for her.

Her friendships with Evelyn, Pax, Callie, Taamira, Skye, and Ava had been one of the multitudes of bounty she'd been blessed with when she'd married Mitch Quinn. But Bebe and Aubrey were like sisters to her, and she loved them as such.

"Stop day-dreaming, Mrs Quinn." Mitch hooked an arm around her waist as he held Maggie on his shoulder with one big hand on her back.

Autumn wrinkled her nose as she grinned at him. "I'm just remembering our wedding day."

His eyes went warm with love for her as he bent to kiss her lips, it still made her heart quicken with desire and excitement. "Best day of my life." He swung Maggie down in front of him, allowing her to toddle in front of them on sturdy legs.

Mitch swung an arm over her shoulders and bent to touch a palm to her rounded belly, at twenty weeks, they'd just found out they were having a son. Neither of them had wanted to wait, too impatient to know the gender of the child she carried. Autumn couldn't wait to see Mitch hold their son in his arms.

His brow furrowed and she lifted a hand to stroke the bristled cheek. "You feeling good?"

"Yes, I'm fine."

He smirked, knowing her too well. "Nervous?"

"A little. This has been a dream for so long, and to be here now is amazing." The truth was her belly was alight with nerves and joy. To exhibit her garden design at the Royal Horticultural Society's Chelsea Flower Show was surreal.

They stopped beside the garden she'd designed with the help of Mimi, David, Reg, Colin, and Ava. Her gardening club buddies had encouraged her when she'd told them her dream had always been to go to the Chelsea Flower Show with her design. She'd filled in the form with her details and forgotten about it until she got the invite to exhibit.

Mitch had supported her one hundred percent, fetching and carrying, shovelling and allowing their home to become overrun with tiny seedlings which she'd nurtured into healthy plants. They had stayed in the house where her life had begun, but now the top floor was one big apartment instead of two.

Maggie liked having her aunty Bebe and uncle Waggs close, and Autumn had wanted that too. She and Maggie had been parted from family and knew what it was to be alone but now she was surrounded by love.

Autumn blinked twice as she saw the gold rosette on the stand next to her name and that of her garden.

Looking up at Mitch with wonder, she gasped. "I won. Oh my god, Mitch. We won." Autumn jumped up and down with pure delight as she threw her arms around the man who owned her heart.

"I'm so damn proud of you, honey." His voice was gruff with love as he bent and kissed her as if it were his job, not caring that everyone could see, not holding anything back. The cheers from their friends and family who'd all come out to support her dimmed when she was in his arms, nothing else mattered when he kissed her.

Autumn kissed him back just as hard, her tongue tasting his love and her body shivering as she thought of the nights ahead with this man.

He released her slowly, and she caught the giggle of Ava and Zack's son, Riley, who Maggie was looking up at with absolute adoration in her little girl's eyes.

Mitch followed her gaze, her chest rumbling with a growl, which made Autumn laugh.

"Easy tiger, they're only kids."

"Yeah, now they are, but one day they won't be."

"And you will have to deal with it."

He bent to pick his daughter up and blew a kiss into her neck, making her giggle. "No boys ever."

"Or girls?" Autumn said with a tilt of her head and grin.

Mitch frowned. "No relationships ever. She's my baby, aren't you, Maggie?"

Maggie laughed and said her new favourite word as she patted Mitch on his head. "Dadadadad."

Looking at the two of them together was her favourite thing in the world to do, and she knew it always would be.

Autumn looked at the people who'd come out to support her, seeing Will and Aubrey and Alex and Evelyn, who had the tiniest baby bump. They'd started trying on their honeymoon and were due three months after she was. Her mum and dad and Rion, Mitch's mother and step-father who she adored. Even Jack had taken the time out from being a workaholic to come and support her.

He walked to her and kissed her cheek. "Congratulations, Autumn."

"Thanks, boss."

Jack chuckled at her use of the term. "So, are you gonna leave us and become a famous gardener now?"

Autumn twisted the silver bangle on her arm and shook her head. "And leave my favourite guys without any order or direction? Never."

Jack held a hand over his belly. "Thank god."

Autumn laughed at his antics. "But I'm taking time off when the baby comes so you need to see if you can get someone to cover me."

"I'll sort it."

"When does Val start?" Autumn asked of their new dog handler.

"Monday morning. The dogs will still be in quarantine, but she wants to get everything set up."

"It'll be nice to have some more estrogen in the building."

Mitch chuckled and guided her back through the garden she'd created, his hand in hers. She leaned into him and sighed with pleasure.

The English country garden, with box hedging, beds of lavender, foxglove, hollyhock, and roses meandered through a pea gravel path. A tranquil Japanese inspired pergola sat at the back with wisteria hanging over it while honeysuckle climbed up the trellis. A nearby stream running through to a statue of cupid on the left had been recreated from her mind and was now a living garden.

He pulled her to sit under the pergola and wrapped her in his arms. "Happy?"

She pulled away, turning to look at him with a quizzical expression, before reaching to run her thumb over his full lips. "I didn't know I could be this happy."

His face lifted into a beaming smile. "When Devon is born, I want us to take a trip to Jamaica so the kids can see where their grandparents were born. I want them to have a sense of where they're from, of who they are."

Autumn's eyes prickled with tears at his words; this man was too much at times. He knew how important it was to her that Maggie and Devon knew where they came from, and he was making it happen.

"I love that idea. Do you think we should ask our parents if they want to come?" That both their mothers had been born in Jamaica had been a surprise. That they were from the same town of Albert an even bigger one. Her mum Shanice, being so much younger had never known Mitch's mum Vea, but now the two women were family through the grandchildren they shared.

His warm chuckle had her body seizing with desire, and she clenched her thighs together. "You want to take our parents on our honeymoon?"

"Think of the babysitting and the long walks along the beach— alone."

"Fine, you've convinced me."

"Good, now let's go home and I can show you how much I love you."

Mitch's lips found hers, and she knew as long as she had his love, her life would be full of beauty.

Sneak Peek: Scarred Sunrise

Smithy and Lizzie's story

He watched from afar as she alighted the vintage Rolls Royce outside St Marys Church. She looked like a vision in froths of satin and lace, the ivory colour only enhancing the radiance of colour in her cheeks. She turned as if sensing him and their eyes locked, and for just a moment he wanted to run to her, sweep her off her feet and take her away. Beg her not to do this, not to marry another man when he loved her with every breath in his body.

The wind blew her veil across her face and the connection was lost and so was the moment. When she lifted her hand to pull the lace away from her features, he saw her falter and knew he was wrong for coming here. He'd wanted to see her one more time before she belonged to another man. It had been selfish, and he could see by the tremble in her lip he'd once again hurt the woman he loved.

As her sister approached her with a bouquet of pink flowers, he stepped back into the shadows. Lizzie looked for him and he saw the wistful longing on her face before she lifted her head, straightened her shoulders, and took her father's arm. Smithy watched until she was inside before he moved down the alley, walking until he found himself outside the Pool Centre.

He looked at the old signs with fondness as he remembered a time when all that mattered was a game with his friends and catching a sneaky snog with whatever girl he was with at the time. Anything to get away from the life he'd lived at home.

Now his life had changed, he'd left the depressing, day in day out slog of caring for a person more intent on their next fix than being a parent to him. He'd closed the door on the woman he loved and would never be good enough for and followed his best friends into the army. Now he had a brotherhood, a family of sorts. A job he excelled at and loved, and a determination to make the best of himself.

He'd walked away to let Lizzie live the life she deserved with a man worthy of her, who'd give her everything good in life. Not a man like him who had nothing to offer except his body and his heart, because that wasn't enough for her.

Smithy sighed and tipped his head to the sun on this day in June when everything changed and the future he'd wanted, craved, disappeared into dust. He strolled past the busy shops; the soles of his military boots silent on the pavement. Taking no heed of the people around him except to ensure they weren't a threat to him, the heat of the mid-afternoon sun making him sweat in his military fatigues.

The car was waiting when he turned the corner to his home, and he felt a calm come over him as he slid in the back seat and the man in the front lifted his gaze to him. The older man wore a plain black suit, his face held an expression as unreadable as a blank sheet of paper. "Smith, are you ready?"

"Yes, sir." He was ready and yet he wasn't because he was leaving half his soul and all of his heart in St Marys Church.

"You know nothing will be the same after this mission, don't you, son?"

Smithy lifted his gaze from the window where the scenery was speeding past the car. "Sir?" Smithy cocked his head in question.

"This life, it changes you in a fundamental way and the mission you're about to take on isn't one that will leave you without scars."

"I understand, sir."

The man looked at him with speculation on his face. Smithy held his gaze not wanting to be taken off this op. It was what he needed; a focus so complete that it would drive all other thoughts from his head. Especially how beautiful his Lizzie had looked today and how, by now, she was a married woman.

"I don't think you have any clue, but you will."

Smithy kept silent as the car drove him towards a future that was uncertain and filled with mystery. He'd embrace this life and make it his own. On this thought he smiled, he finally had a chance to shine, to prove to all those that had doubted him, had looked down on him, that he was worthy. That he could make a difference in this world and not end up a strung out junkie or serve time for petty crimes that would lead to bigger ones.

He wouldn't become a statistic in this world. He may have been born poor and weak but now he was strong, and he had enough money to keep him in what he needed.

The car slid to a stop and he saw two men standing beside a small aircraft that would take them to an unknown location. He recognised Fitz, a man from his unit, and hid his shock as he alighted the vehicle and pulled his Bergen from the boot.

He and Fitz lifted a chin to acknowledge each other before he did the same to the unnamed man. He didn't know his name, but he knew his face from the barracks.

"Gentlemen, this is your last chance to back out. From this point forward, until this mission is complete, you'll be subjected to things that will leave a mark of you, that will scar so deep it will be tattooed on your soul."

Smithy felt a second of doubt, a moment he would later wish he'd heeded. But with nothing left to lose, he walked up the steps of the aircraft and towards a future that was so dark he wasn't sure he would ever see the light again.

Books by Maddie Wade

Fortis Security

Healing Danger(Dane and Lauren)

Stolen Dreams(Nate and Skye)

Love Divided(Jace and Lucy)

Secret Redemption(Zack and Ava)

Broken Butterfly(Zin and Celeste)

Arctic Fire(Kanan and Roz)

Phoenix Rising(Daniel and Megan)

Nate & Skye Wedding Novella

Digital Desire (Will and Aubrey)

Paradise Ties: A Fortis Wedding Novella (Jace and Lucy & Dane and Lauren)

Wounded Hearts (Drew and Mara)

Scarred Sunrise (Smithy and Lizzie)

Zin and Celeste: A Fortis Family Christmas

Fortis Boxset 1 (Books 1-3)

Fortis Boxset 2 (Books 4-7.5

* * *

Eidolon

Alex

Blake

---

* * *

Alliance Agency Series (co-written with India Kells)

---

* * *

Ryoshi Delta (part of Susan Stoker's Police and Fire: Operation Alpha World)

* * *

Tightrope Duet

* * *

Angels of the Triad

* * *

Other Worlds

About the Author

Contact Me

If stalking an author is your thing and I sure hope it is then here are the links to my social media pages.
If you prefer your stalking to be more intimate, then my group Maddie's Minxes will welcome you with open arms.

General Email: info.maddiewade@gmail.com
Email: maddie@maddiewadeauthor.co.uk   .
Website: http://www.maddiewadeauthor.co.uk
Facebook page: https://www.facebook.com/maddieuk/
Facebook group:
https://www.facebook.com/groups/546325035557882/
Amazon Author page: amazon.com/author/maddiewade
Goodreads:https://www.goodreads.com/author/show/14854265.Maddie_Wade
Bookbub: https://partners.bookbub.com/authors/3711690/edit
Twitter: @mwadeauthor
Pinterest: @maddie_wade
Instagram: Maddie Author

Printed in Great Britain
by Amazon